BEN'S STORY
NORMAN TEBBIT

BEN'S STORY
NORMAN TEBBIT

Illustrations by Debbie Mason

Bretwalda Books Ltd

www.BretwaldaBooks.com
@Bretwaldabooks
bretwaldabooks.blogspot.co.uk/
Bretwalda Books on Facebook

First Published 2014

Bretwalda Books
Unit 8, Fir Tree Close, Epsom, Surrey KT17 3LD

info@BretwaldaBooks.com
www.BretwaldaBooks.com

ISBN 978-1-909698-72-7

Cover design & typesetting: dkbcreative
www.dkbcreative.com

AUTHOR'S NOTE

This is a story about how a boy called Sam, his help dog Ben and their friends avenged the death of Sam's father. It is a work of fiction, but many of the places, not least the dog school at Canine Partners do really exist.

None of the characters are real but those who knew the late Daphne Parkes, who was a brave and distinguished MI6 secret agent in Russia and Africa, may think that Sam's friend Alice Bacon is just a bit like her. As for Sam, sadly there all too many boys who suffer severe spinal injuries and have to cope with life confined to a wheelchair.

Sam's friend Ben is a yellow labrador like many of the help dogs trained at Canine Partners, and perhaps he is quite a lot like my dear old friend Ben. My Ben was as faithful as the one in this book and although he could not communicate as Sam's dog does in this story, he often knew what I was thinking and I often knew what he was thinking too.

The real life Canine Partners is based near Haywards Heath and the help dogs they train are truly wonderful animals who help hundreds of people live full lives despite all sorts of injuries and disabilities.

Norman Tebbit

CONTENTS

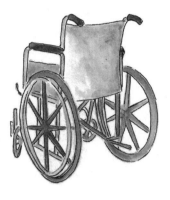

CHAPTER ONE

STOKE MANDEVILLE HOSPITAL

The boy lay awake in his hospital bed in the spinal injuries unit at Stoke Mandeville. It is never quite dark in hospital wards and he could see the humps in the beds where other patients were sleeping, and the clock on his bedside locker. It was still only 3 am. Time always dragged in the hospital, especially at night.

Before long it would be different. After six months Sam knew he would soon be going home again – but nothing at home would be the same. He was not the same. He would never walk again. Nor would he ever see his father again. His father was dead. His life – everything – had all changed in those moments when the car swerved off the road, down the bank and hit the tree. And now nothing could ever change things back again. What had happened had happened. That was that. Sam could not remember much about the crash, until he found himself in the hospital bed with tubes in his mouth and nose and bottles of blood hanging on frames over his head. It had been a terrible nightmare of people shouting, blue lights flashing, stretchers, fire engines, the ambulance men lifting him out of the wrecked car. He remembered asking, *"Where's my father? What happened to him?"* but no-one had told him then that his father was dead.

It had been bad enough when his mother and father had parted. He worked very late and sometimes he was away for days at a time. She said he was never at home. He said that was what it was like if you wanted to be a top crime reporter on TV. Then one day his mother took Sam and his sister and they left to live in George's house a couple of miles away. Sam's mother thought he was great, but Sam and his sister were not so sure. Being a teacher was bad enough, but he was well, just boring and their father had been well, not always there, but when he was, anything but boring. He was fun.

Now it would be far worse. Sam's father would never again be there to take them out to fun things like films and concerts and football, or even museums.

On the night of the crash he had taken Sam into London to see a film – a real thriller about how gangs smuggled drugs and sold them – even in schools like his.

"Stop it" said Sam to himself before he could begin to cry. "I can't change what has happened. But I can change what might happen next". That is what Mr Shah, the chief surgeon at the Spinal Injuries Unit, had told him on his first day in hospital. Perhaps Shah was a bit like his father. He could not spend much time at home either. He was always at the hospital working. As if in answer to his thoughts, Sam heard Shah's footsteps. He always wore proper shoes, not trainers and the heels clicked on the hard ward floor in the quiet of the night. Sam turned and lifted his head to watch him and Shah stopped beside his bed.

"What are you doing here in the middle of the night?"

"What are you doing laying awake in the middle of the night?" they asked each other.

"Another motor car accident Sam. I had to see what we could do for him. It is really my day off so I didn't think I would see you". He half chuckled at the thought of a day off. "Then I thought, I would bet Sam's awake – so I looked in to tell you the good news. You will be going home very soon".

"Thank you" said Sam. "I want to go home – but I'm a bit scared and I'm worried".

"Of course you are. Only fools don't worry and only fools are never scared.

But you will be alright. I'm sorry we could not mend your back – that is still impossible at present, but we fixed all the other broken bits as good as new. You've got your eyes and ears, your nose and tongue, your brain and your arms and hands..."

Sam interrupted him. *"That's all very well, but how about going to school? I won't be able to keep up with my friends – I'll just be left on my own."*

Shah sat down on the bed and put a hand on Sam's shoulder.

"Let me finish Sam. I know what you have lost and I know what you have got left. I shouldn't tell you this, but I will. The young man they brought in here tonight is dead. I couldn't save him. You're alive. Being at home will be hard at first. You have made friends here. There are plenty of others like you – but you'll be the only one who can't walk at home or at your school. I know you will be lonely at first so I've spoken to an old friend of mine. I want you to go to see him because I think you should have one of his dogs..."

Again Sam interrupted him. *"How can I look after a dog...?"* And again Shah interrupted Sam. *"No Sam – you won't look after him. He will look after you. He will be trained to be your friend, your helper – even your bodyguard – they call dogs like that canine partners. Now Sam. That's enough. We will wake everyone up and I'll get the blame. You will hear from Clive Baker at Canine Partners in a week or so asking you to go to see him and hear about your new friend. Now get back to sleep."*

And before the night nurse could give him another warning look, Mr Shah was gone. Sam closed his eyes to shut out the world. He hated to see the wheelchair beside his bed.

When he woke up again it was getting light and the morning rush and bustle of the hospital ward had started. Why do they start so early wondered Sam. Then once you are up nothing much happens for hours. But today would be different. His mother would be coming to take him to see his new bedroom and bathroom at home. By mid-morning he was up, ready and waiting for her and as she came into the ward he grabbed the wheels of his chair and propelled himself across the floor to meet her.

"Mum – I'm coming home – and Mr Shah says I'm going to have a dog. Is that alright?"

CHAPTER TWO

SIBERIA

A t just about the time that Sam was telling his mother about having a dog to look after him it was late afternoon 4000 miles away in Siberia.

It gets dark early there in October, but the man laying in bed was too weak to reach out to switch on his bedside lamp.

"Nikita" he called. *"Nikita"*.

A younger man came in. *"What is it Boris? Can I help?"* he asked.

"Help me up in bed. There are some things I must do. Put on the light and get me some tea or soup. I feel cold".

Nikita lifted Boris' shoulders, propping him up with the pillows, pulling the blanket up around his shoulders and going around the room, switching on the lights before closing the curtains.

"I'll get some soup" he said.

As he left the room the big yellow Labrador uncurled from the rug in front of the wood stove, came across to the bed, then standing on his hind legs looked deep into the eyes of Boris.

"It's no good Ben" said Boris. *"I will soon be gone and you must find a new life. You can't stay here. If the authorities found out our secret there is no*

knowing what they might make you do. We Russians don't understand dogs – well, we do in a way – but not like the English. So you must leave here – very soon – perhaps tomorrow".

Ben's head dropped – his tail hung between his legs. Then looking up at Boris, Ben let his thoughts form inside Boris' head – just as though he was speaking out loud.

"But Master, I can't leave you. You need me with you. Please don't send me away. What would I do without you? Where would I live?"

"Poor Ben. You must know I am very ill. Before long you will be on your own anyway and I want you to go now while I am still here to protect you and before it is too late. You must go to England."

"England Master? I know you lived there once, but you have never told me about it – or where it is. I have overheard some of the other people here talking and I'm not sure they like England."

Boris turned his head away as Nikita came into the room with his soup.

"Be quiet Ben, get down," he said. Nikita smiled as he gave Boris the tray.

"He doesn't mean it Ben – he thinks more about you than anyone else."

But Ben looked away, making just one of those grumping noises which Labradors do – and which might mean anything.

As the door closed again behind Nikita, Ben looked up again at Boris, then without a word came back to stand beside his bed again.

"Listen carefully Ben" whispered Boris. *"You must go tomorrow. Nikita will take you."*

"But where Master – and who will look after you?"

"Don't worry about me. Nikita's sister can stay here. I will be alright. At least she will be able to call the doctor or the priest. As to where - I told you, to England. You know that I love England and I almost became a defector to stay there when I was a student at Cambridge University – now don't look so worried, I'm not sending you to study at Cambridge.

Boris began to laugh, but chuckles turned to coughing and Nikita came into the room.

"Are you alright?"

Not quite able to speak Boris nodded, then as Nikita hesitated he got back his breath to say *"Yes – I just thought of something funny".*

13

Nikita looked from Boris to Ben, who hid his face in his paws – then back to Boris.

"If you're sure – alright then" and picking up the tray, he went out and closed the door.

After a moment or two, Ben looked up again. *"Yes"* he said, in a way that turned the word into a question.

Boris took a deep breath. *"Ben, you know that I listen to the BBC, the British radio."*

"I do Master, but you know that I cannot understand the radio. Well, only a few words – but it is not like hearing your thoughts as you speak in my brain."

"Quite so" agreed Boris, *"but let me tell you about a programme that I heard a year or so ago. But first of all remember, you must never let anyone here in Russia know of your gift. All dogs can receive in their brains the tiny electrical signals humans make in our brains when we speak. But you are different. You receive them so well that you hear what I am saying in my brain and when you reply the signals are so strong that humans can hear you inside their heads. You are so different – almost a unique dog, that even when you get to England you must be very, very careful who you tell until you reach your new home."*

"My new home Master – but where will that be?"

"Come close" said Boris. *"Come up on the bed. I will not speak out loud – I will just think my words in a whisper."*

Ben needed no second invitation. Does any Labrador hesitate when asked to get up on a human's bed? He was still there an hour later when Nikita looked in to see if Boris was alright.

"Ben! What are you doing? Boris, that dog should not be on the bed."

"Oh Nikita – he is my friend and these days now that I am no use as a nuclear scientist I've not got many friends. Let him be."

Nikita shook his head and turned to go, but Boris raised his hand.

He paused and looked at Nikita, who took a deep breath. *"Boris, I owe you so much – just tell me what you want me to do..."*

Their eyes met and then Boris began.

"Nikita, Ben is a very special dog. Please don't ask me why. Of course he is my friend, but it is more than that, and you know that we Russians are not like

the English. The English treat their dogs like people and I'm afraid all too often we Russians treat people like dogs. But that is beside the point. Ben would have a better life in England and I want you to help him get there."

"But Boris" argued Nikita, "it's a long way from here to Moscow, nearly 1000 miles, let alone to England. How on earth..."

Boris raised his hand and interrupted Nikita's question.

"There is an envelope in the top drawer of my desk. There is some money in it – plenty of money in fact. Take that to pay your fares and to bribe the police and any officials who might otherwise hold you up. Use it to go to Poland."

"To Poland – Where? Why?"

"Nikita just listen. I am very tired and I must tell you tonight because you must leave in the morning. You must go to Gdansk. It is a Polish seaport on the Baltic Sea and there are small freighters which go from there to the small ports on the South or South West coast of England. Get Ben smuggled on board. Make sure he is on the ship. Make sure it is going to England and made sure the crew do not know he is on board."

Boris saw from his face that Nikita was more doubtful.

"But Boris – it will not be easy – more likely impossible. And what about Ben? How will he know where he is going?"

"All very good questions Nikita" said Boris. "But you must trust me as I trust you. Don't worry about Ben. Just use the money to get him on the right ship and you will have done your job – and neither I nor Ben will ever forget that."

The two men fell silent and Ben who had sat absolutely still except for his eyes which had flicked from one to the other, gave just three short barks – then licked first the face of Boris and then Nikita's hand.

"Off the bed Ben," ordered Boris. Then "Nikita would you help me? It is time I had some sleep – and so should you and Ben. You need to be away early to catch the train to Moscow."

It was still dark next morning when Nikita opened the bedroom door to call Ben, who had hardly time to jump up onto Boris' bed and say goodbye.

"Nikita – have you got the money, plenty of warm clothes, your travel documents and food for Ben? Oh, and would you tell your sister I'll sleep on for another hour."

As Nikita left the room the eyes of Ben and his master met.

"*Goodbye Ben*".

"*Goodbye Master – must I go and leave you?*"

"*Yes – it is for the best. Remember all I told you. Keep our secret. You are a very special dog.*"

A last touch of hand and paw and Ben was down out of the door without looking back, to start his long journey to a new life. In moments Nikita had put Ben on his lead, swung a great rucksack onto his back and they were tramping over the frozen snow to the gates of the research station at Sarov, a place so secret that for many years its name was not on the Russian maps. The guards knew Nikita and they scarcely looked as he waved his papers and walked on towards the station.

It was a relief to find the train was on time and they settled into an empty compartment. Ben curled up behind Nikita's feet – almost under the seat – and prepared himself for the long journey to Moscow.

The last door slammed shut. The train drew out and Ben realised he would never see his master again. What neither he nor Nikita knew was that Nikita would never see Boris alive again. As the train was pulling out for Moscow he had closed his eyes and taken his last breath.

The massive dose of radiation which he had received in an accident preparing the test of a Russian nuclear bomb years earlier during the Cold War had finally killed him.

For a while the silence in the compartment was interrupted only by the clackety-clack of the wheels on the railway tracks. Then Nikita put his hand down and gently stroked Ben's ears.

"*Ben*", he said quietly. "*Ben, I never told you nor Boris, but I know The Secret of your Gift. I understand why you have to leave Sarov and get to England. If the authorities knew your secret I know, and Boris knows, they would use you to go into the most terribly dangerous radioactive places. Boris and I remember the terrible accident at Kystya in 1957. That was long ago when Boris was only a pup, but his father never really recovered and died when Boris was still young. Then it was another accident here at Sarov which let loose the radioactive gas which caused Boris' illness. Lots of dogs in your family have been ill too. Some were born with terrible things wrong with them. His did not want that to happen to you and he believes that in England you will find a safer life.*"

CHAPTER THREE

ARRIVAL IN ENGLAND

It was one o'clock in the morning, it was raining and the gutters were full as the rain flowed back into the sea along the docksides of the little Devon port of Teignmouth.

The man locked his office door – he had been working late going through the papers for the Polish freighter 'Gdansk'. She had only arrived that day, but her captain was anxious to leave on the high tide due at four in the morning and with the papers finished the man's job was done and he walked towards the gate in the fence around the docks. Sitting patiently, soaking wet, blocking the gate was a large dog – a pale yellow almost white Labrador.

"What the hell is a dog doing here?" he muttered the words to himself, as he approached the dog. There was something odd about it. It didn't move. It sat like a stone dog simply blocking the gate. It wasn't threatening. It looked neither hostile nor friendly, but its deep brown eyes looked back unblinking straight into his. Again he muttered as much as he thought the words, *"What is he doing here?"*

"Waiting for you to open the gate". He felt the words forming in his mind as though the dog had spoken to him.

There was something strange about the dog. Where had it come from he wondered?

Dogs were not allowed on the dockside.

"I came on board the 'Gdansk'. Again the words came into his mind in answer to the question.

The man looked around. Although he wasn't quite frightened, he wished there was someone else in sight – but there wasn't. He was alone with the dog. He spoke loudly in his most commanding voice,

"Come on dog. Move over."

Again the reply came into his head. *"I will, if you would let me out."*

It was as if the dog understood every word he said – and as if he heard the dog inside his head.

Am I going barmy? he thought. Perhaps he had been overworking. Or had he fallen asleep at his desk – perhaps it was just a dream?

But the rain dripping down his neck was real enough – and so was the dog.

"Come on man. I'm cold and wet and hungry. The English love dogs and I need help."

There wasn't any doubt about it. The dog was talking to him.

"Alright, I'll let you out – just move over."

"Thank you. What about something to eat? I've been hiding on that boat for nearly a week and I need food."

The dog's eyes never left his, but it moved enough to let him by to unlock the gate. Man and dog went through the gate together and walked along the street side by side in the rain.

By now the man was careful not to talk inside his head. If he thought silently in his mind it seemed the dog could not read his thoughts – but nor could he read the dog's mind either.

About thirty yards along the road the man stopped by his car, pulled out the keys, pressed the remote unlocking button to open the door. But the dog was quicker than him. In less than a moment he was in the driver's seat of the car, his head trained to look once again straight into the man's eyes.

"For God's sake – get out – get out" he yelled, losing control. Why had the dog picked on him? Was he dreaming? Was he going mad? Suddenly he was afraid.

The words came into his head again.

"I am hungry – and cold. And I need help. Come on – a dog is a man's best friend. If you'll take me home – I'll move over."

It was absurd – a weird nightmare or delusion – but it wasn't. It was real. There really was a talking dog – sitting on his seat in his car and he was standing in the rain.

He hesitated. *"Well, I'er, I..."*

The dog cut him short. *"Come on – get in"* and he moved into the seat well by the passenger seat.

The man got in, looked at the dog and began to laugh.

"I'm going mad – I must be mad. Dogs can't talk. This is crazy."

"Not really. Unusual, but not crazy. There have never been many of us, but in my family some of us can communicate with people. We can't speak. You don't hear me through your ears. We talk to each other in our minds. But only if you want to."

The man said nothing. He kept his thoughts unspoken. What the hell was he going to do? He couldn't wake up his wife and tell her he had brought home a talking dog. She would say he was mad. Anyway there were her cats.

He started the car, then looked at the dog. *"Alright. I'll take you home. You can stay in the car in the garage. I'll find you something to eat. But you can't stay with me. We've got three cats."*

"I know that" said the dog. *"I can smell them on your clothes – but thank you."* Man and dog fell silent as the man drove through the rain. It wasn't far to his home, where he drove straight into the garage, got out and as the dog followed him, turned and said in his most commanding voice, *"Stay"*.

To be on the safe side he closed the garage door behind him. Within minutes he was back with two tins of cat food, a bowl of water and another containing the lamb casserole his wife had left for him in the kitchen. The casserole went in a flash and he tipped the cat food into the empty bowl. That went too. Then the dog stood up to him, paws on his chest.

"Thank you."

The words came into his mind. *"I'll sleep here"* and it gave his face a lick.

Trying not to think in words, the man opened the garage door – but then couldn't help himself from saying, *"Goodnight – but what's your name?"*

"Call me Ben – what's yours?"

"I'm John. Goodnight Ben."

"Goodnight John" came the reply.

John closed the door behind him, not letting himself even think until he was safe indoors. He poured a drink, shook his head and asked himself again, *"Am I going mad? Have I really brought home a talking dog? And given it my supper?"*

Upstairs, he slid quietly into bed beside his wife – and unexpectedly fell sound asleep.

The man John woke at about six o'clock as it got light and as quietly as he had slipped into bed, slipped out, put on a dressing gown, crept down the stairs and out to the garage.

He stopped at the door – hoping desperately that it had all been a crazy disturbing dream and nothing more. But it wasn't. As he stepped into the garage he saw the dog, still asleep and sprawled across the back seat of the car. What now? Should he take the dog to the RSPCA or the police?

"What am I going to do with him?" he said half aloud. Ben stared – stretched – shook his head and stared straight back at the man John. The words formed in his mind.

"I need to go to Midhurst."

"Midhurst – where's Midhurst?"

"How would I know? I'm Russian. I've never been in England and I can't read – but I know it is in Sussex wherever that is."

John got into the car and pulled out from under his seat, his road atlas.

"Midhurst" he muttered, running his finger through the index. *"Page 12, square D44. Ah – it's about ten or fifteen miles north of Chichester and that must be one hundred and fifty miles from here – or as you're Russian, say about two hundred and fifty kilometres."*

"How can I get there?" asked Ben.

"Well, I'm not taking you. You got here from Russia, so you can get another one hundred and fifty miles."

Ben stretched out again on the back seat. *"Well then, I'll have to stay with you. Would the cats mind?"*

"Never mind the cats – how do I tell my wife and my friends I've adopted

a talking dog? Why don't you leave me alone?"

There was a long pause and at last Ben dropped his gaze, his head dropped and ears fell even more limply over his head.

"Because I need your help and I need to go to Heyshott, which is near Midhurst."

"Look" said John, *"you're not my dog. I didn't invite you here. You just can't stay and I can't take you to Midhurst. I've got to go to work."*

"So have I – I've got to go to work in Midhurst."

There was another long pause and John realised time was going by – his wife would be awake and even worse, so would his children. If they knew about Ben they would never want him to go. He had to make a deal to persuade the dog to leave.

"Alright then. I'm sure there is a bus from Exeter to Chichester. I'll take you to the bus station in Exeter and that's it. You'll have to work it out for yourself after that."

"But I can't pay the fare" said Ben.

"Well, you got here without paying the fare so you'd better do the same again. Look, please, I've done my bit to help. I should have turned you into the police. You might have rabies or something like that."

"If I had, I might bite you – but you're right. Take me to Exeter – then I'll find my way."

"Then stay here until I go to work. I'll drop you at the bus station. If you get arrested you'll have to pretend you're just a dog. If you start talking to the police, they'll never let you go."

Dogs not only can't speak, they can't laugh or smile – but somehow Ben's face changed. He very nearly smiled.

"Thank you."

Just before nine that morning the Polish freighter 'Gdansk' was rounding Start Point heading into the South Western Approaches on her way back home.

The Captain yawned as he turned to the First Officer. *"I'm tired. I was up late doing paper work. I'll leave her to you."*

"OK, Skipper. Everything looks fine – and I haven't seen that dog. I'm sure there was one on board and I'm pretty sure he jumped ship. It was strange.

Sometimes I could have been sure I could hear a voice – it wasn't one of the crew – and it couldn't have been the dog..." His voice trailed away in embarrassment.

The Captain looked at him. *"You must be crazy. Whoever heard of a talking dog, stowing away to get to England as an illegal immigrant? But I think I might be crazy too, because I sometimes thought I could hear someone talking when there wasn't anyone there."*

"I thought I was going crazy too. But it's stopped now. I can't hear it."

"If there was a dog on board" said the Captain, *"he is in England now – and he is someone else's problem. I'm going to bed."*

The ship's cook had brought them their breakfast and was standing close enough to hear the conversation. He smiled as he thought of the bundle of notes in his pocket that a man called Nikita had paid him to smuggle the dog on board.

And Ben was indeed someone else's problem. The man John had stopped by the kerbside. He leaned across to open the front passenger door; Ben uncurled himself, stretched and turned to look at him.

"This is it" said the man. *"The entrance to the bus station is just around the corner – but I don't know how you'll get on on your own"* and he opened the front passenger door.

"Nor do I" said Ben. *"I'll just have to find another human as helpful as you. Thank you."*

As he stood up – the dog turned back and licked the man's face – *"Goodbye."* And he was off, tail wagging, amongst the people scurrying their way to work.

"Now, how does a dog without any money get onto the bus to Chichester?" Ben asked himself. *"I know, I need another man."* He walked around the station watching. *"Got it."* It was sheer inspiration. As the man sitting on the seat laid down his neatly rolled *Daily Mail* newspaper beside him, Ben squeezed behind the seat and deftly took it into his mouth and trotted smartly along the street.

"That's the first stage," he mused. *"My master always said men could go almost anywhere on the military camps in Russia so long as they look confident and carried a bundle of papers."* But now he needed another human. He chose the middle aged man neatly dressed in country tweeds. Saying nothing, he

fell into step, just behind him as close as any most perfectly trained dog would walk to his master's heel.

Ben sized up the bus station and began to regret that he had not asked the man for rather more help. There was no problem about getting in, but how would he discover which was the bus for Chichester? The noise from the public address loudspeakers was incessant and unbearable, but it was to Ben just noise. He could not understand a word of it. Nor could he read the notice boards, nor the signs listing the destinations of the buses.

Ben's Russian master had often told him, *"Don't draw attention to yourself. If you do some wretched official will take an interest in you – and that is usually bad news. Make yourself part of the background."* Boris' words came back to Ben's mind. *"Don't let anyone even notice you – unless you want to."*

Ben noticed there were no other dogs around and realised he would have to find another helpful human, but they all looked busy, carrying cases and bags. *"I'll have to take a chance"* he decided. He had taken refuge under a seat to keep out of the way and moments later an elderly lady struggling with her case gave him a smile as she sat down. Ben stayed quiet as a moment later a young man wearing jeans, sweatshirt and trainers, took the other end of the seat. The elderly lady shifted nervously and the man, sensing her anxiety, said in a pleasant voice, *"It's much nicer today after all that rain isn't it?"*

"Oh, yes" she replied, relieved at his polite tone. *"Especially for travelling."*

Ben thought hard. *"Are you going far?"* he said, directing his thoughts to both of them.

"I'm going all the way to London" said the lady, as the man said,

"I'm off to Bristol."

No help there , thought Ben. *"I wish I were going to Chichester."*

"Chichester?" said both the young man and the elderly lady.

"I really don't think I've ever been there" she added.

"Nor me" said the man. There was a long pause. *"Did you ask about Chichester?"* said the man.

"No. I thought it was you."

"How odd! Please excuse me. I mustn't miss my bus," and looking very uneasy, the young man got up and walked away.

Ben took a deep breath. *"I'll have to own up."*

"*I'm sorry about that. I hope you were not upset or embarrassed.*" The words formed out of nowhere in the lady's mind.

She looked around. There were dozens of people hurrying by – but clearly none of them had spoken to her. What is going on – am I going silly or hearing voices she thought.

"*No, no, you're quite alright*" said Ben. "*You're not imagining voices. It's me, the Labrador under the seat.*"

It was too much for her. She turned and saw Ben, wagging his tail, one paw raised.

"*Oh, no! There is a dog there.*" She gathered up her bags, stood up, dropped them and sat down with a thump.

"*Oh, I am sorry, really I am – but I do need help.*" Ben put his paws on her lap. "*Please, help me. It's me that wants to go to Chichester.*" He gazed up at her – as appealing as only a Labrador can be.

She went to speak, but Ben interrupted her. "*I've got no money. I've never been to England before. I'm a refugee, but I know where I could find friends. Please, help me.*"

"*This is mad – dogs can't talk, but I can hear what you are saying – it's not possible.*"

"*Oh, yes it is. But I won't explain. It is too long a story. I need to get the bus to Chichester. Will you help?*"

"*But I can't. They don't allow dogs on these buses – not even with someone and certainly not alone, and I'm going to London to see my sister. I can't take you to Chichester.*"

Ben's ears and tail were drooping. How, he wondered, would he ever find Clive Baker whom Boris had said would help him in England. He felt ashamed that after all that Boris and Nikita had done to get him to England, he had no idea what to do next.

The old lady looked at him. Ben had no need to speak – his body language told her what was in his mind.

At last she opened her big leather handbag, searched inside, pulled out a digestive biscuit, pretended to be about to eat it – then offered it to Ben. He hardly had time to thank her before it was gone, but it jolted him out of his gloomy mood.

"Now" she said. *"Tell me exactly where you want to go."*

"I have to find a man called Clive Baker. He has a school for dogs."

"Where?" she asked. *"At Chichester?"*

"No – Boris said that was the nearest big town."

"So what will you do when you get to Chichester?"

Ben realised that the lady might look very old and frail and rather vague, but she had an air of authority. He did not know, of course, that she too, had a secret about her life. She had often been in danger and she knew how to deal with fears and doubts.

Ben realised that he had come close to panic and despair at being lost with no idea what to do next.

"Do you have this man's address?" she asked quietly.

"Yes – er, No – er. No – I did, but I've forgotten."

The old lady spoke very softly. In fact, not aloud at all. She just formed the words in her head – but, of course, Ben could hear her.

"Fancy sending a dog off on his own to find someone. What was his master thinking of?"

"It wasn't his fault," said Ben. *"My master, Boris, is very ill and he said I had to escape from Russia. He only knew about Clive Baker because he heard him on the radio."*

The old lady stared at him harder than ever.

"You have come from Russia? And your master expected you to remember an address in England and find your way there? I just don't believe this is happening – I must be dreaming."

A passing couple saw the dog – one paw on the old lady's lap and heard her speaking excitedly to him – but they just smiled and walked on. Slightly batty old ladies do sometimes talk to dogs out of loneliness, so they did not even bother to hear what she was saying.

"No." Ben told her. *"No – you're not dreaming. I am a real dog. I have come from Russia."* Then suddenly he remembered what Nikita had told him on the train. His words burst into the old lady's mind as though he had shouted in her ear and several other people nearby jumped as words came from nowhere into their heads too.

"Of course – I'd forgotten. Nikita wrote it down on a piece of paper and put

it in a locket on my collar. Is it still there?"

He stood up with both his front paws on her lap to let her feel around his collar.

"Yes – it's there".

She released the catch and took out the neatly folded paper and read aloud. *"Clive Baker, Canine Partners, Mill Lane, Heyshott, Midhurst, West Sussex. That is where you need to go. Oh, I do wish I could take you there, but I can't. And you are a lost dog."*

Ben remained silent. He did not really understand how humans found their way about the world. Nor do we understand fully how a dog can follow another animal's tracks – or find his way back home by scent or the tiniest whispers from the Earth which "educated" people need compasses to interpret, but some Australian aboriginal people can still feel and understand.

Ben did not like the idea that he was a lost dog. It made him feel very insecure and he wished he was back in Russia with his master, Boris.

The old lady looked from the address on the paper to Ben and back to the paper again – and then a smile lit up her face.

"I've got it – Yes – I know how to get you there. But what is your name?"

"I'm Ben – Ben."

"Good," she said. *"Come with me – we are going to the pet shop."*

Pausing only to leave her heavy bag at the left luggage office, she set off briskly out of the bus station with Ben puzzled, but impressed by her air of purpose at heel.

Within minutes they were in a shop like Ben had never seen before. His senses were almost overwhelmed by the sights and sound – but, of course, most of all the smells. Dogs learn far more about the world around them by scent and far less by sight than we humans do. Ben lifted his head and drew in air over the scenting cells in his nose, where he could separate each scent, savouring them all and then one at a time identifying most, thought some were new to him. There were wonderful dog foods, where he could smell turkey, chicken, lamb, rice – oh, and there were doggie chocolates and chews and treats. Then there was the scent of cage birds and some kittens – even young puppies. Of course he could see the food packets and the birds and animals in cages – but not in such colours as we would see – rather more like an old black and white film on TV, and he could hear some sounds which people cannot hear.

Fortunately, Ben remembered his manners and tempted as he was to rush around the shop investigating every scent, he sat beside the old lady just quietly sniffing as Labradors do. He then realised the old lady was speaking to an assistant.

"I need a new dog identity disc for Ben. He has lost his old one."

Within a few minutes they were leaving the shop and Ben was wearing his new disc with his name and address – "Ben – Care of Clive Baker of Canine Partners, Heyshott, Midhurst, West Sussex."

"Ben," she explained. *"We are going to the police station."*

Ben had his doubts. Boris had told him, *"Never get into the hands of the police if you can help it, but if you do, never, never let them know the secret of your gift. Listen to what they say – but don't say anything."* He hesitated – then sat down on the pavement and gave a half bark, half whine.

"Come on," said the old lady. *"Come on boy. If I tell the police you are a lost dog, then they will look at your disc and let Mr Baker know you have been found."*

Ben still sat – his backside almost glued to the pavement.

The old lady sighed. *"Now, come on Ben. You really do not have much choice. Either you trust me or you're on your own again. You've been lucky so far, but your luck night not last. The police here are not like the police in Russia, but your master was right to tell you not to let too many people know your secret. Just pretend to be an ordinary dog. The police will look after you. I promise they will."*

Ben was thinking hard. She was right. He did not have much choice – and his luck might run out. He looked very hard at the old lady and she heard in her head the quietest of whispers.

"Alright. Thank you. I will not say any more."

Before long, they were in the police station with the old lady telling the duty police officer she had found Ben lost and alone at the bus station.

Of course, that was not strictly true. Ben found her, but she thought it best not to say that.

Within a few minutes PC Hudson had looked at Ben's new disc, taken down all the details, filled in a form and with a smile thanked the old lady.

"May I have your name and address please?" he asked. *"Oh, yes – I am Miss Alice Hanson and I live at 27 Old Church Road, Exeter."*

"Well, that's it," said PC Hudson. *"Thank you for bringing Ben in – I'll phone our people at Midhurst. They will get Mr Baker's number and let him know Ben is here. Oh, did you have his lead?"*

"No" replied Miss Hanson. *"He didn't have one."*

"Hmm" remarked PC Hudson. *"You must have a way with dogs."*

"No, no officer" said Alice, as she turned to leave. *"I think Ben has a way with people – I'm only sorry I could not keep him."*

Ben had to try quite hard to avoid saying anything. Instead he looked straight at her – and with a very quiet bark, wagged his tail.

PC Hudson had come out from behind his desk and took Ben by his collar, leading him through a rear door across the yard behind the police station towards a kennel and dog run inside a wire netted enclosure. As PC Hudson opened the gate, Ben's heart sank. He had never been put in a kennel. He had always slept beside his master, Boris' bed.

He almost said, *"but can't I stay with you in your office,"* but remembered just in time not to let anyone else know his secret until he found Clive Baker. Instead he dropped his tail and ears, sat down and whined looking pathetically at the man.

"Come on Ben," he pleaded. *"It's alright."* But Ben remained as glued to the spot as only a large dog can be. Hudson tried a half hearted tug on Ben's collar and realised the dog was too heavy to shift.

"Alright then – come back to the office. I'll phone Midhurst and get you something to eat."

To his surprise, Ben stood up – wagged his tail and walked ahead of him back into the office, stood up to the desk, lifted the phone handset off the rest and offered it to him, just as he would have done for Boris back in Russia.

PC Hudson was still standing with the phone in his hand looking at the dog when another officer came in.

"Hello – what's this? A stray dog?"

Hudson nodded. *"More of a strange dog than a stray dog. I swear he understands everything I say. I said I would make a telephone call about him and he handed me the phone."*

"Well" laughed the other officer. *"We could do with some help. You'd better ask him if he'd like a job?"*

"I don't know about that – I'd better make this call to ask the boys at Midhurst to go round to his owner to say we've got the dog here."

Listening to the call, Ben began to get anxious, wondering what Clive Baker would do when the Midhurst police told him that his lost dog was at Exeter police station. Baker had never heard of Ben and might just say he had not lost a dog – and what then? But he was not only anxious about that. Ben was hungry and he could smell food. A couple of sniffs told him it was a cold beef sandwich – no pickles – just butter on brown bread. Two more sniffs and he knew it was in the desk drawer with an apple and a bar of chocolate. He put one paw on the police officer's leg, then went and sat with his nose at the drawer and gave a sharp bark.

Hudson looked at him – then opened the drawer and saw the sandwich.

"That's mine – but I'll find you some dog food." After a moment or two, searching in a cupboard, Hudson came back with a bowl of food and another of water.

"Boris was right," thought Ben. *"The English police are different,"* and he emptied both bowls and curled up under the desk.

Realising that Ben must be lonely and worried, Hudson left him under the desk. But the dog was not the only one to be worried. Alice Hanson, the old lady, was back at the bus station. She had missed her bus and was busy texting her sister in London to say she would be late, but her thoughts were about Ben.

She looked again at the receipt from the pet shop for his name disc and the form they had given her at the police station. No, she wasn't losing her mind. That dog could communicate in words straight into her mind.

"Extraordinary," she thought.

Miss Hanson was not just any old lady. She had been in the Secret Intelligence Service and had heard rumours that the Russians were trying to train dogs and dolphins to communicate. It was odd that he had told her he was Russian. What was he up to? Suppose Clive Baker said he had not lost a dog? What would happen then? Perhaps she would claim him – but that wasn't what Ben or Boris, his master, had wanted. And then she had a terrible thought. What if Ben was not being honest with her? Could dogs lie and deceive like people?

Who was Clive Baker and what was Canine Partners? It sounded very odd. All her training in the dark world of spies and intelligence began to tell her she could not just hope all was straightforward and would be well. She would have to phone Clive Baker. It was only 4 o'clock and he should still be in his office. The bus was less than half full and she took out her mobile phone, dialled directory enquiries and in a few minutes was through to Canine Partners asking for Clive Baker.

She told his secretary she was an old friend who needed to speak to Clive Baker and she put her call through. A puzzled Clive Baker confessed that he could not remember her.

"Of course not Mr Baker" she assured him. "We have never met, but I wanted to let you know you will be getting a call from the police about your lost dog, Ben."

"But, Miss Hanson," he protested, "I haven't lost a dog called Ben."

"Quite so," she interrupted him. "It would be more correct to say that Ben is looking for you. He is a truly remarkable dog. I can tell you that he has come on his own from Russia to find you. I know you are thinking I am a batty old lady, and old I may be – batty, I am not. I have not led a sheltered life and I have never met a dog like him."

"From Russia? To find me? That's a bit unlikely isn't it Miss Hanson?" he asked.

"You'll find out about that – and it gets more unlikely than that. You must go to get him without delay. Thank you for saying you will."

"I didn't say I would," protested Clive Baker.

"No, but you will, I know" said Alice, and turned off the phone leaving Clive with a very uneasy feeling that something odd was going on.

Within moments his secretary came in to tell him the police were on the phone. It was about a lost dog Ben. He picked up the phone as though it might bite.

"Clive Baker here."

"Hello, Mr Baker. Good news for you. Your dog Ben has been found in Exeter. He is fine, but obviously missing you."

Clive drew a deep breath. *"Oh – good – wonderful. I'll go down tomorrow to pick him up. Exeter you say? However did he get there?"*

"Well Sir, he was taken into the station by an elderly lady," the police officer explained. *"She found him at the bus station. I must say, you're lucky to get him back. The boys at Exeter say he is a very smart dog. I will tell them you'll see them tomorrow. Goodbye."*

Clive Baker put down the phone. *"What is going on?"* he thought and shook his head.

How did his name get on the identity tag of a dog he had never heard of? Anyway why should Miss Hanson have telephoned him to say that the police had the dog and were going to phone him? What was it she said? That the dog had come from Russia – on his own – looking for him?

Like almost everyone who had met Ben, Clive Baker wondered for a moment if he was going slightly batty. He decided there was only one thing to do. He would go to Exeter the next day to find this unusual dog. Until then he would say nothing.

"Jean" he called to his secretary. *"I've got to go to Exeter tomorrow. It is about a dog who might just be what we want for training for one or two of the people we've got waiting for dogs. So I won't be in the office."* Having settled that, he got back to work and put Ben out of his mind. It would be the last time for quite a while he would be able to do that.

Back in Exeter, Ben had been keeping his head down. Everyone seemed to have accepted that he should stay under the desk in the front office of the police station. Both Boris and the old lady, Alice Hanson, had told him to keep his secret to himself, so he just listened to all that was going on. Not that he understood most of it, so he just dozed quietly in the way that dogs can. They look to be asleep until some sound or scent – the smell of food or something unexpected like smoke – will wake them in an instant. In just the same way, they will sleep through all sorts of noise, but wake in an instant at the sound of their master's footsteps or anything which might spell danger.

At 2 o'clock police had changed shifts and PC Hudson had handed over to Steve Brown, explaining that the police at Midhurst would be getting in touch with Ben's master, Clive Baker, at Canine Partners. *"They know Clive Baker quite well,"* he added. *"He runs a training centre for dogs to help disabled people. If they are all like this one I think we could do with one here. He seems to understand every word I say. Anyway, if I were you, I'd leave him where he is. He's no trouble, although I suppose he might need a walk."*

Ben had been listening and thinking that might be a good idea, got up and walked to the door.

"See what I mean," said Hudson. *"I'll take him, but I suppose he ought to be on a lead. We mustn't lose him."*

Ben sighed. He hated being on a lead, but he needed to go out. Where, he wondered, would they have put a lead? Perhaps in the cupboard with the food and dog bowls? He walked to the cupboard, pushed his nose up to the gap under the door and sniffed deeply. Yes – he could smell leather and the scent of another dog. That must be a lead he thought and rattled the door. Hudson and Brown looked at each other. Hudson opened the cupboard. Ben stood up with his paws on the shelf and took the lead. Ben had his walk and settled down again under the desk where he stayed till morning to the relief of Steve Brown, who felt slightly uneasy about this strange dog.

At the Victoria bus station in London, Alice Hanson also had some explaining to do. Her sister, who had come to meet her, enquired what had delayed her in Exeter?

"Oh – I had to deal with a lost dog," she explained.

"A lost dog? Why did you have to look after him?"

Alice replied without thinking first. *"Well, he asked me if I would take him to Midhurst, but of course I couldn't do that, so we went to the police station...."* and then Alice fell silent, realising that she had said too much.

And perhaps she had. Her sister gave the old lady a very strange look and said no more. But later that night she told her husband she was worried that Alice was beginning to lose her mind. *"She told me that a dog asked her to take him to the police station."*

"Hmm. She's lucky they didn't keep her in," muttered her husband and promptly fell asleep.

By then it was still less than twelve hours since Ben had arrived in England, and already he was leaving a trail of people wondering if they had had a very odd dream, were losing their minds or if they had really met a most extraordinary animal?

CHAPTER FOUR

CANINE PARTNERS

At 8 o'clock the next morning Clive Baker was turning out of his drive and heading for Exeter grumbling to himself about the rush hour traffic. However much he tried not to keep asking himself why a lost dog in Exeter had his name on his collar his mind kept coming back to that question. What was it the police officer had said – he was *"a very smart dog."*

Well, thought Clive, if he is, then wherever he has come from, perhaps he could be trained as a "canine partner."

There was never a shortage of disabled people of all kinds who needed a trained dog to help them, and now his old friend, Shah, the senior consultant at the Stoke Mandeville spinal injuries hospital had asked if he could find a dog for Sam Pearson. Sam was fourteen years old. His parents had parted and Shah had told him that as if that was not bad enough, his father had been killed in a car crash which had left Sam paralysed from his waist down. *"He needs a friend – a real friend that he can always trust,"* Shah had said. *"The people in his life have let him down. He needs a dog - one of your dogs - and he needs it now because he is leaving hospital very soon and he feels very lost and lonely."*

It was all very well for Shah to say the boy needed a dog, but dogs take time to train and every dog at Canine Partners anywhere near ready to start work was already allocated to someone. But perhaps if Ben really was smart, he was the answer. After all, what had the old lady, Miss Hanson, told him? That the dog had come from Russia to Exeter, met up with an old lady and landed up as a lost dog in the police station?

After a while Clive Baker gave up asking himself questions he could not possibly answer and got on with his journey to Exeter.

It was not quite 11 o'clock as he turned off the A30 into Exeter and followed the signs to the police station.

For some reason he felt slightly nervous as he walked up to the desk and asked for PC Hudson.

"Yes," said the clerk. *"Can I tell him what it is about?"*

"Of course. I've come to collect a lost dog. My name is Baker."

The clerk's face lit up. *"Oh, you mean Ben – he's a lovely dog – but however did he get all the way here from Midhurst – it must be one hundred and fifty miles?"*

One hundred and fifty miles – if Miss Hanson was right, it was more like three or four thousand miles, thought Clive Baker, but he kept the thought to himself and just smiled.

"Well, that is a mystery I must say," he observed. *"But where is Ben now?"*

"Right here, under PC Hudson's desk," replied the clerk. *"Hi Ben – your master's here."*

Ben had been listening carefully to make sure he didn't make a mistake. He had been working out how he would recognise Clive Baker and how he would greet him. Now was the time to do it. Out from under the desk, paws up on the counter (he couldn't jump over it because of the glass screen) and Ben let out a series of half barks, half whoops of welcome, looking straight into Clive Baker's eyes.

By now PC Hudson had arrived and opened the door to let Clive Baker into the office, but Ben was too quick for him and in a moment was through the door, standing up on his back legs and paws on Clive's chest to give him a big licking.

"Well," said Hudson. *"I don't have to ask if you two know each other."* Just as

well, thought Clive – and so did Ben, who dropped down onto all four paws and then sat at heel by Clive's right side.

Within a few minutes the paperwork was done. Ben had barked his thanks to PC Hudson, wagged his tail and followed Clive out of the door, along the road and into the back of his car. Clive turned in his seat and looked at the dog.

Ben returned his gaze. Eventually Clive broke the silence.

"Ben – you are a strange dog. Are you really Russian? You look like a pure bred English Labrador to me. How do you know about me? Wherever you've come from, why have you come to me?"

Ben almost started to answer, then thought better of it. There were a lot of questions in his mind too and he could not help thinking about his master, Boris and Nikita. They had warned him to be very careful about letting people know his secret, so it was probably best to say nothing, but listen a lot. He dropped his head and curled up on the floor ready for the last part of his long journey from Siberia to Midhurst.

Dogs are not people and they do not think like us. Because he used words as we do, Ben could think about far more things than other dogs, but unlike us, he simply did not think about all the possible things that might happen tomorrow or next week. Perhaps that is why dogs are usually more relaxed about life than people. Lying on the floor in the car, Ben thought that so far, since Boris had sent him to England, he had managed quite well. He had found Clive Baker and he was on his way to Canine Partners – the school for dogs that Boris had told him about.

What Ben didn't know was that the old lady had telephoned Clive to make sure that he would drive to Exeter to claim him as a lost dog, or that she had told him that he had come from Russia.

He soon picked up scents of several other dogs from Clive Baker's clothes and he thought they smelt quite good, but there really wasn't much more he could do, so Ben did what Labradors do extremely well at such times – he tucked his nose into his paws and went to sleep.

As the car turned onto the motorway, Clive was still going over and over in his mind the mystery of how his name and phone number had come to be on the identity disc on Ben's collar. Why had the old lady taken the dog to the police as a stray and how did she know he had come from Russia? Suppose Ben had rabies? Could it all be some terrible terrorist plan to bring that dreadful disease into Britain? He'd better keep him away from the other dogs until the vet had seen him.

More and more, as the miles passed by, Clive began to worry and to wish he had never let himself be sucked into pretending that Ben was his dog.

Ben was dreaming about his life with Boris in Russia, when through his sleep, he sensed the rhythm of the car changed. The sound of the engine had changed as they entered Midhurst, slowing in the traffic, accelerating as they left the town and then slowing again as Clive Baker turned into the lane leading to Canine Partners headquarters. Taking his nose out from his paws, Ben let out a great gulping yawn to let Clive know he was awake, and stood up to look out.

It looked a bit like the military camp where Boris lived and worked thought Ben. Several office buildings and large barns with grass and tarmac areas rather like parade grounds. And there were other dogs, but not on their own. Every dog was with a human. Most of the dogs wore yellow jackets and some of the humans were in wheelchairs.

It all reminded Ben of the schools where they trained dogs for the Russian Army and to work on the nuclear experimental sites. Clive's voice interrupted his thoughts.

"Well Ben this is home for you for a few weeks at any rate," said Clive as he parked the car. *"Come on – let's go to the office."*

"More like go for a pee," thought Ben, as he got out of the car and headed for a tree. Nose in the air, he sniffed deeply. *"Wow – there are at least a dozen dogs round here."* Having left his mark, Ben turned and followed Clive into the main office building.

Clive's secretary, Jean, looked questioningly at him and then at the dog.

"Well, who is this?" she enquired. *"What's his name?"*

Ben almost replied without thinking, but just managed to give a friendly bark instead.

"This," said Clive, *"is Ben. I'm told he is a remarkable dog, but so far he hasn't done much but sleep."*

Ben was a bit hurt at that, so he put his paws on Jean's desk and gave the nearest he could to a smile.

"To tell you the truth – and please don't tell anyone else," Clive continued, *"there is something very odd about him. He was taken into Exeter police station as a lost dog by an elderly lady, who said she found him wandering around the bus station. The odd thing is, he was wearing a tag with Canine Partners, my name and this address on it."*

Jean put her hand on Ben's paw and looked at him.

"He doesn't look as though he has been a stray. Perhaps he needs a brush, but I think he is a very handsome Labrador – but you're right, it is all a bit odd."

Clive walked back to the door and made sure it was shut.

"It is even more odd than that. Promise me you won't tell anyone this?"

"Of course," Jean said at once.

"Well, - you know I had a call yesterday afternoon from a woman who said she was an old friend...."

"Yes," Jean reminded him, *"but she didn't have much to say to you. She was on the phone for less than a minute."*

"That's right – Miss Hanson, she said her name was, and she told me that the police would be ringing me about my lost dog. I told her I hadn't lost a dog and she said, no – but he was looking for me – and he had come from Russia. I told her that was a bit unlikely and she said it would get more unlikely than that, and rang off."

Jean looked back and forth between Clive and Ben.

"There is something about him. He is absolutely calm and he watches us as though he understands everything we say."

"All the better," observed Clive. *"Shah at the Spinal Injuries Unit wants me to find a dog for a boy called Sam who is fourteen years old and from a broken family. His father was killed in a car accident. The boy had his back broken and will never walk again. He needs a dog and we haven't got one anywhere near trained that isn't already promised to someone and, as you know, we don't normally give dogs to anyone younger than eighteen. But Ben might be the answer. I'll take him home tonight. We had better get the vet to see him before he mixes with other dogs, and then start his training. Give the vet a call – tell him I'll bring Ben in tomorrow morning – just say he's a new dog. Nothing more."*

"*Right*" said Jean, as she closed the door behind her.

Clive turned and looked out of the window. Several dogs were doing their basic obedience drills with the trainers. It all looked well ordered and tidy which, as an ex-Royal Marine officer, Clive liked.

"*Oh, Lord – I just have that feeling there is trouble coming. I don't like being in something I don't understand. Someone must have decided this dog should come here – but why? They must have wanted him to train as a help dog, but why couldn't they bring him here? Perhaps they knew we don't normally take adult dogs because it's harder to train them.*"

Once again, Clive Baker realised he was asking himself questions he couldn't possibly answer.

He sat down at his desk, looked at the pile of letters to be signed, tried to read the top one, realised that he wasn't taking it in at all and put it back on the pile. After a few moments more of just moving the papers around on his desk, Clive got up.

"*What on earth is wrong with me? I really wish I had never said that dog was mine. There is something odd about him. Perhaps I'm going mad.*"

Suddenly, in his head, he heard someone speaking.

"*I'm sorry Master – I really didn't want to leave my Master Boris – but he told me it would not be safe to stay in Russia without him and he was very ill. I'm sorry to be such a problem.*"

Clive swung round to look at the dog.

"*What did you say?*" Even as he spoke the words he felt a fool. Had he really thought the dog had spoken to him?

Ben dropped his head and stared at the floor. He had given away his secret without thought – and what's more, sounded sorry for himself – what a fool he felt.

"*I really must be going mad. I really thought that dog was speaking to me,*" Clive muttered to himself.

Ben lifted his head – and as he always did when he had something important to say, he looked straight into the man's eyes, got up and put a paw on Clive's leg. In the softest whisper he formed his words.

"*No, Master – you are not going mad. I was speaking to you. I am an unusual dog and that is why my Master Boris sent me to you. Although I can't speak aloud like you, I can – if I try – let you hear me in your brain – and I can understand you."*

Clive Baker sat down abruptly and a bit annoyed.

"Why didn't you tell me this before now?" he asked.

"My Master Boris told me to be careful about who I told. He said, not all humans would look after me if they knew my secret, but he had heard about Canine Partners on the BBC World Service radio and he thought I would be safe with you."

In all his years of fighting in wars around the world, in all his years of training dogs, Clive Baker had never felt so utterly unsure of himself – or what to say – or what to do.

"Ben," he said. *"I need to think about this. I'd best clear up here and take you home. In the meantime – just stay quiet."*

He sat down at his desk, looked once more at the pile of letters to be signed, but none of them made any sense to him.

"Jean," he called out, and then as his secretary opened the door, *"Jean, I've had a long day, so I'll head for home. I'll take Ben with me and I'll take him into the vet tomorrow on my way here."*

Out of the corner of his eye he noticed that Ben had already got up and headed for the door.

Neither man nor dog spoke on the journey home. Clive Baker's mind was churning over and over again the events of the previous twenty-four hours. Ben was wishing that he could be back in Russia with Boris and Nikita. The last ten days had been a roller coaster of fears and hopes. He just wanted it all to stop and life to be normal again.

Clive parked the car on the drive of his house and with Ben at his heel, opened the door and walked in. Like many servicemen – especially Marines and SAS men who spend many years going from one of the world's trouble spots to the next – Clive had never married and lived alone, but the house felt warm and friendly Ben picked up the scents of other dogs and food. Sure enough, there was a casserole in the oven for Clive's supper and a glow from the wood burning stove looked inviting.

Clive looked at the note from his housekeeper. Ben opened his nostrils and sniffed at all the scents in the house. He knew from that just as well as

Clive did from reading the note that a woman had been in the house and his ears told him she was no longer there. Nor did he have to read the note to know that there was food in the oven. A chicken casserole and a jacket potato.

Clive put down the note, went to the cupboard, took out a bottle and poured himself a drink.

"*Whisky,*" sniffed Ben. "*That's what Boris used to drink,*" and guessing what would happen next, he went and sat beside the big armchair that smelled of Clive, by the stove.

Clive looked at him and laughed.

"So, you make yourself at home then Ben. Look, I still think I must be dreaming or going mad. Dogs can't talk. It isn't possible."

As he always did when he wanted to say something important, the dog put a paw on the man's knee.

"*Master, you are not going mad. You are not dreaming. I am real. Of course you are right. Dogs can't speak. I can bark and growl and things like that, but I can't speak and you don't hear me through your ears. It is as I told you. You hear me in your brain.*"

Before Clive could say anything, Ben carried on explaining how the heavy doses of radioactivity had affected many people in the Russian nuclear weapons and power research station where his master Boris had worked.

"*I do not understand these things, but whatever this radioactivity thing is – you can't smell it or see it, but it can kill people – and dogs too. Sometimes they sent us dogs into terrible places where men would not go. It did not just kill people and dogs or make them ill like my master Boris – it made our puppies ill too. Sometimes they were born with only three legs – terrible things like that. In my family some of us were born able to hear – or smell – or something – I do not know the word for it – people speaking in their heads, but I think I am the only one who did not die of the terrible radiation sickness.*"

Clive just let Ben talk. Suddenly, it made sense. When our brains are working there are tiny electric currents in patterns that can be detected and measured. Dogs can sense some of those patterns – which is how 'help' dogs can warn a person with epilepsy before they are going to have a seizure and collapse. Ben's words were still forming in his brain.

"My Master Boris said that I was a special dog because I could hear in my head what he was saying and I could make him hear in his head what I wanted him to know."

"My Master Boris had this radiation stuff – it made him very ill. He told me that he would soon be dead and that I could come here and you would find me a new master. Then he told his man, Nikita, how to get me onto a ship that would bring me to England and then I would have to find you. I was very frightened, but I am glad to be here."

Clive took a large sip of his drink. This was the most extraordinary story he had ever heard. If Ben was telling the truth (and anyway, could a dog lie?) Boris had put Ben in his care – so he really could not let Boris or Ben down.

"Dear Lord," he thought. *"Why have I been landed with a Russian talking dog?"* He soon realised that above all, he must not let Ben become a celebrity dog – exploited by television and showbiz. If Boris had sent him to Canine Partners because he had heard the BBC programme about 'help' dogs, then Boris wanted Ben to find a new life as a 'help' dog. But what did Ben want?

That, thought Clive, is not so easy. Dogs aren't people. Not even talking dogs. A good Labrador can do many things people cannot do, but dogs are not clever in the way humans are. He had always thought that a good Labrador was about as intelligent as a two or three year old child, although a child of two or three would not live very long on its own without other people, but a dog could.

And, if Ben uses words to think, Clive reasoned, he – like a child as it grows up – might become more intelligent. For certain, if we humans did not have words to think with and to communicate with each other, our thinking might not get very far.

"Ben," said Clive, *"you are safe with me. I will keep our secret as long as you want me to do so. But what do you want to do?"*

"Master – dogs do not live on their own. We live with people. I need to be with a human – to be his friend. I would be your friend, but first of all, I am hungry and I am thirsty. It is long past time for my dinner."

Clive realised that he too, was hungry and within minutes, his plate was on the table and Ben's bowl on the floor. They ate in silence until Clive began to tell Ben what it meant to be a 'help' dog – a Canine Partner. He explained what his dogs did, how they learned to help their human partners get out of bed, get dressed or go shopping, put washing into and out of the washing machine; answer the 'phone, open the front door, pick up things dropped on the floor and so many things.

"It takes about two years for an ordinary dog to learn how to do all these things Ben," said Clive. *"How long would it take you?"*

"Well Master. I used to help Boris do many things like that and if you tell me – or show me – what you want, of course, I could learn quite quickly."

"How about two weeks?"

"Two weeks Master – I could try – but I have only been here a little while and I would like to get to know you and the other dogs."

"Yes – I understand that," said Clive, *"but I know of a boy – he is only fourteen years old. His father was killed and he was badly injured in a car crash. He cannot walk – he lives in a wheelchair. He needs a friend – a special friend. Would you be his canine partners?"*

"Master – I am a dog. My Master Boris said I should trust you. Of course I would try."

Clive got up from the table, walked into the kitchen, opened the door, opened the box of 'Dog Treats,' and offered a couple to Ben.

"Here Ben – that's settled then. I'll get the boy to come to see us. Now I'm going to watch television..."

"Then I'll go to bed," interrupted Ben. *"Dogs can't see what you see on TV. It is just a flickering mess to me. Where do you want me to sleep?"*

CHAPTER FIVE

BEN GOES TO SCHOOL

Clive Baker was wide awake well before his alarm was due to sound at 6.30.

"God," he thought as he woke. *"What a weird dream that was about a talking dog."* And then he realised he hadn't been dreaming. He swung out of bed, slipped on a dressing gown and went down to the kitchen to make tea as usual – half hoping that it had been a dream and that he wouldn't find a dog down there. But he did.

Ben, still curled up by the big Aga cooker, opened an eye, but kept his head down waiting to see what would happen next. Clive, playing the same game, ignored the dog, filled the kettle, put a teacup, saucer and jug of milk on the tray and turned on the radio. Perhaps because they remain closer to their past thousands of years ago when they were hunters than man does to his hunting days, dogs are usually more patient than humans and Ben won the waiting game. Clive gave in and spoke first.

"Good morning Ben. Did you sleep well?"

Ben sighed. Humans did sometimes ask silly questions. Why on earth should a Labrador not sleep well? If there is nothing better to do, then a Labrador will simply close his eyes and take a nap.

"Yes thank you," he replied politely. *"But I would like to go out for a moment – and could I have some breakfast please?"*

Clive opened the door and as Ben sniffed the air before strolling down the garden, he thought there is no doubt about it. Ben might be a very unusual Labrador, but he certainly was a Labrador. Clive found the dog food, poured some into a bowl and put it down beside the water bowl on the floor, then watched Ben exploring the garden, head down, tail up wagging confidently, sniffing around the plants.

A few minutes later whilst Clive was making his breakfast toast, a sharp bark told him that Ben was waiting to come in. In moments he hoovered up his breakfast and curled up under the table as Clive buttered his toast.

The waiting game continued. To anyone watching it would have looked like any well mannered dog at his master's feet waiting to see what the day would bring. But this was different. Man and dog were both wondering just what would happen that day.

Eventually Clive pushed his plate away, finished his tea, got up and walked over to his fireside chair. Ben stayed put.

"Come on Ben," he said at last. *"We have to decide what happens next."*

"Yes Master. You told the woman, Jean, I should see the vet. There is no need for that. I'm quite fit. I got here from my Master Boris' home in Siberia and I'm ready to start to work for you – but if you wish, of course we will go to the vet – but please don't tell him my secret. You spoke about a boy. You said he needed a friend and helper. Is that what you want me to do?"

Clive drew a deep breath.

"I'm beginning to think that it might be better if you came to work in my office. You don't seem to forget much that I say do you?"

A deep furrow formed on Ben's head, running from between his ears right down towards his eyes as he looked doubtful and puzzled. "Dogs," thought Clive, "even one like this, are not people and they do not find it easy to know when people are joking or being quite serious." He hastened to put Ben's mind at rest.

"No, it's alright old chap. I was only joking, but you are good at remembering things." That, of course, is only half true. Dogs do not try to remember as

many things as people do. They really don't spend much time thinking about global warming, whether the grass needs cutting or where to go on holiday, so they remember more of what they do think about, like where they buried a bone or who has dog treats in his pockets and which clothes their masters' wear according to whether they are going to work or out for walks.

"Look, I think we should go to the vet. He will need to give you some jabs to make sure you don't catch nasty things like hard pad or worse. Then we will go to see some of the other dogs at the training school. I do think it might be best if you wanted to help the young boy Sam, but we will have to see if you and Sam agree. And for the time being we will tell no-one of your secret."

Ben looked relieved. He still found it hard to be without Boris.

"Thank you Master – I'll wait for you here."

Ben stayed put – until he saw Clive pick up the keys to the car and then in a moment he was at his side. Clive looked at him and grunted.

"Come on – it's time to see the vet."

The visit to the vet did not take long and by 10 o'clock, Ben had his inoculation certificate and was at Clive's side in the office at Canine Partners. The vet was puzzled that such an intelligent, well cared for dog, should have been abandoned as a stray. But he had assured Clive Baker that Ben was in good health and free to mix with other dogs.

"I think it's time we found out if Ben has got what it takes to be a canine partner," said Clive to his secretary. *"I'll take him over to meet Steve Judge. Come on Ben."*

Together they walked across the yard where half a dozen dogs were with their trainers, and some with their prospective human partners too. As Ben had noticed the previous day, the dogs all wore yellow jackets and several of the people were in wheelchairs.

Clive led the way into an office marked, "Head of Training." The man seated at the desk got up to meet them.

"Good morning Steve – this is an interesting new dog. He came to me as a lost dog – but I think he somehow decided for himself to come to join us. He's very smart and I thought he might do for that boy Sam – the one that Shah, the doctor at the Spinal Injuries Unit, says needs a real friend and helper. What do you think?"

Steve looked intently at Ben.

"He might be too old to train. Come here Ben – let's look at you."

Ben sat at Steve's feet, looked up and put a paw on his leg.

It did not take Steve long to check that Ben understood all the basic words of command, and began testing him by hiding things and getting Ben to find them. After a few minutes he turned back to Clive.

"You're right. He knows what he is doing Clive. Would you go back to your office and I'll send him to you when we have done."

Clive turned to Ben. *"Stay here Ben, with Steve. Do what he tells you – Good dog."*

Within half an hour Clive's secretary, Jean, was on the 'phone to tell him that Steve wanted to talk to him. Clive smiled to himself and asked her to put him through.

"What do you make of Ben? Is he up to scratch?" Clive asked.

"Up to scratch? I tell you Clive. There is something spooky about this dog. I swear he understands every word I say. He's sitting here now – just looking at me as though he understands what I am saying to you. I showed him some of the dogs in training and he could follow any of the commands they were being taught. He doesn't need much training. All you have to do is to tell him what you want. Where on earth did you find him?"

Clive said what was becoming second nature to him to say, *"I didn't find him. He found me. An old lady took him into Exeter police station and told them she found him loose in the street, but he had a name tag with my name and address on it. I thought he was pretty bright, but I wanted to know what you thought. I think we could introduce him to the boy."*

Steve sounded a bit doubtful. *"That's all very well, but what about the boy? How bright is he? What does he know about dogs? How much training will he need? Most people need a couple of weeks."*

"Good questions Steve. I'll have to see the boy. Now – would you tell Ben to come and find me."

Steve laughed. *"Tell him yourself – I'll give him the 'phone."*

"It's a funny thing Steve. He doesn't seem to understand the 'phone or the radio or TV any more than other dogs do. You have to actually be with him. Ask him to find me – go on." And Clive put down the 'phone.

In no time at all Ben was at the door. Man and dog looked at each other. Clive laughed. Ben wagged his tail; he did not need to be told he had passed his first test at Canine Partners.

Clive closed the door and beckoned the dog to come to sit beside him at his desk. Quietly, so that Jean in the room next door would not hear, he spoke to Ben.

"You did well. You heard what Steve said about you – but be careful Ben. We don't want everyone to guess your secret. They have to think you're a very smart dog – but not to realise just how different you are."

Ben took the hint. It was only his eyes and tail that told Clive he had heard him.

For several minutes Clive sat staring first at the dog, then the blotter on his desk, then out of the window and then back at the dog. What the hell should he do. He wished again it was all a dream – but it wasn't. More like a nightmare! He was in his office. The dog Ben was real. He could communicate.

The problem was, what to do? The boy Sam needed a dog – but did he need Ben? Weren't there more important things Ben could do? Wouldn't he have wanted a dog like Ben when he was in the Royal Marines fighting the IRA, or in South America breaking up drug smuggling gangs? Perhaps he should call his friends in the Ministry of Defence. It was Jean's knock on his office door that brought Clive back from his thoughts.

"Come in," he called out. *"I was just thinking about what would be best to do with Ben. I really don't know..."* His voice trailed off as he looked from Jean to Ben, out of the window and back to the dog.

"Clive," she said. *"I've never known you like this about a dog before. What's the matter? I thought you wanted him to go to the boy Sam – the boy Mr Shah rang you about."*

Ben stayed silent. He let his front paws slide forward until he was stretched out on the floor, his chin resting on his paws. *"People,"* he thought. *"People were strange animals – much more clever than dogs, but sometimes they made a big fuss out of very little things."*

Clive did not like a girl to see him dithering. He had to make up his mind and take a decision.

"We had better contact Shah and get the boy's details – his full name, age, 'phone number and all that. You could e-mail him. You know what we need and then I'll see the boy."

"So, it's all down to me as usual," thought Jean. Of course that is what she really liked about the job. Clive might be in charge – but really nothing would get done without her.

"Okay," she said. *"Leave it to me."* And Clive did.

CHAPTER SIX

SAM AT HOME

Sam had been home for a week and it wasn't getting much better. He was glad to be out of hospital and trying to live a normal life again – but it wasn't normal and it would never be again. He <u>was</u> a cripple – they told him not to say that word, but that was what he was. A cripple. He could not run, nor even walk nor stand up and his world was full of barriers now that were not barriers before, and weren't barriers to other people. Stairs, steps, narrow doorways, rough steep ground – and cobbles – bloody cobbles and bloody high kerbs. Everything took more effort and more time; even getting up and going to bed. And worst of all, most of the boys he had thought were his friends simply couldn't be bothered to wait for him or help him.

People had simply changed, mostly for the worse. Not his sister Sophie though. She was great. A year older than him, she used to be just silly or bossy and never thought about anything except girl things, but now she made time for him. She noticed when he needed help and did things without saying or making a fuss. Sophie was good.

But his mother hadn't changed. He could never forgive her for leaving his father and he had always hoped she would go back home – to their real home with his father – but now she never could. Somehow she seemed sort of mechanical, Sam thought. She looked after him, got his meals and helped him with his clothes, but she didn't seem to understand he was fourteen and didn't want his mother dressing him. Anyway, he would have to learn to do things for himself and though it had been embarrassing at first, he would really rather ask Sophie for help if he needed it.

As for George – he had been a real surprise. He hadn't liked George. He had stolen Sam's mother from his father and broken up their home. And he was a teacher. And he was boring. Yet it was George who had fixed things. He seemed to understand what Sam needed. The house where they lived was quite old and a bit higgledy-piggeldy and George had always had the best room in the place as his study, but he had moved out and made it into a bed-sitting room for Sam.

Sam's emotions still swung sharply – sometimes he was depressed and sad – he even wondered if life was worth living at all – and then suddenly something good happened and he was sure that he could overcome his injuries. It had not been easy on his first day back at school. He didn't want people to be sorry for him, or treat him differently, but it would be nice if they didn't let doors swing back in his face. Games were pretty awful. He knew he could cope with most things, but he was still glad to get home every day, just to get away from other people.

That day – the day Ben arrived at Canine Partners – was the day that George had told him about the break-in at Sam's father's flat.

"Look Sam," George had said. *"There is something you should know about your father."*

Sam felt a flash of anger. What business was it of George's to tell him what he should know about his father? He almost told him to mind his own business – but then saw from George's face that he was uncomfortable about it too.

"Yes," he said doubtfully.

"Well, it was all a bit odd I think – but the police were not very interested. When we – your mother and I – went to your father's flat a few days after the accident – we had the keys because the police had given them to your mother – we found it had been burgled. We didn't know until we opened the door – it was

locked and there was no sign of a break-in – but someone had been in and it looked as though the place had been searched. His computer had gone – all his papers had been turned over and the books were all turned out onto the floor. The rugs had been turned up and the cupboard and drawers turned out and his music centre turned over too."

Sam broke in – "What about his books? He always told me some were quite valuable..."

"I can't be sure – but it didn't look as if many had gone and I found several that I knew were valuable, but we did not know exactly what he had. It didn't look like an ordinary burglary – it looked as if someone had been looking for something."

"What has happened to the flat now?" asked Sam.

"Well," said George. "It's not really my business to tell you that. That is between you and your mother, but what I can tell you is that we – that's including Sophie – thought you should have your father's discs and tapes – you know there are loads of them. So you've got some storage units for them coming tomorrow. And I'll take you to the flat if you would like and we'll pack up the discs and tapes."

"Thank you George," mumbled Sam. "I really am grateful to you – but what did the police say?"

"Well, they said there had been a lot of break-ins around there – mostly people on drugs looking for money or easy to sell valuables – and they really didn't seem that interested."

"Drugs," thought Sam. "Drugs – it keeps coming back to drugs." He knew his father had been following a story about one of the biggest drug suppliers.

"They are the scum of the earth," he had told Sam. "But, they are not common criminals – they are not flashy or anything like that. They live in nice houses – they have plenty of money – they cultivate responsible friends, they give money to charities and they never touch the drugs themselves – but they give the orders and they take the profit. And the profits come from the addicts who kill, rob and steal to find the money to buy their drugs."

George could see that Sam was deep in thought and waited until he turned back to him. Sam's eyes were not really focussed. It was as though he was looking inside himself rather than at George.

"Sam – you know I'll always help if I can, but I don't want to interfere. Just let me know if there is anything you would like me to do."

"I think I would like to go to the flat," muttered Sam. Then he almost shouted in anger. *"But how would I get up those bloody steps to the entrance doors?"*

George could have kicked himself for not thinking of that. Neither he nor Sam had adjusted to Sam's new more limited world.

"Sam, I'm sorry – I feel such a fool. I should have told you. While you were in hospital the Council made them put in a ramp."

"No-one told me. It's always the same," shouted Sam. *"Let's forget it. I'm sorry. I've got enough on my plate getting to school and getting around. It's no bloody good George – I just can't keep up with the others and most of my friends – well, they used to be my friends – now they can't be bothered. George, I can't give in. Mr Shah told me off for being sorry for myself and I'm doing it again. He's right. I've still got my eyes and ears, my nose, my tongue and my brain – it's only my bloody legs that don't work. It won't beat me."*

"I'm going to – to – to do things. I don't know what – but I'll do something – I know I must."

There was another long pause – then Sam remembered what else Shah had said.

"He said I needed a friend – a true friend. He said I should have a dog friend and he said I would hear about it soon. Has Mum said anything about it George? I wanted a dog before, but she said it would be too much bother – and who would look after it and all that. She's not said 'no' without telling me has she? George – tell ..."

Sam realised that the words were gushing out without him thinking what he was saying and he stopped in mid-sentence. He was utterly miserable and he almost began to cry. He was suddenly afraid of the great black wave of misery that threatened to overwhelm him. Above all, he knew he must not cry in front of George. He must not give in. He must not give in. He shut his eyes tight and swallowed hard.

Shah was right. He did need a friend who would always be utterly completely loyal – a friend who would never tell if he found him crying. A four footed friend. Before George said anything more he swung his chair round and left the room without another word.

CHAPTER SEVEN

SAM GOES TO CANINE PARTNERS

It only took Jean a day to arrange the 'phone call for Clive to talk to Sam.

"Sam," he said. "I think I've found the right dog for you. He hasn't finished his training yet – but I don't think that will take long. I've known a lot of dogs, but he is the cleverest dog I've ever known. I would really like to keep him, but if he decides he would like to be your partner – then he's yours."

Sam hardly knew what to say.

"Mr Baker, that's wonderful – but I'll have to talk to my mother – and my stepfather – and there's school and ... and ... and ... But when can I come to see him?"

"Pretty well when you like," Clive replied. "Look, why don't you talk it over with your family and decide when you would like to come here? I'll send you some forms and a map of where to find us and all that. Is that okay?"

Sam hardly had time to say, "Yes, and thank you," before Clive Baker put the 'phone down and looked round at Ben who had been sitting looking at him.

"Ben," he said. "It's time you started work for a new master".

It was George who drove Sam to meet Clive Baker and Ben at Canine

Partners. They talked very little. Although Sam had come to realise that George was something of a friend and a lot more understanding than his own mother, he was still the man who had ousted his own father, and so in Sam's mind he was partly responsible for his death. For his part, George respected Sam's feelings and tried not to intrude, but eventually as they approached Midhurst, he broke the silence.

"Sam – what do you expect the dog to do?"

There was a long pause. *"I don't think I know. Mr Shah said he would be my friend, whatever happened, and my helper – yes – I remember he said even my bodyguard. Sometimes, George, I could do with that. Some people think that because I can't use my legs, I can't use my brain and they try it on. Perhaps they wouldn't if I had a dog."*

George nodded as he overtook a slower car, then turned again to the boy.

"I've talked to your mother and you know she wasn't keen about you having a dog."

Sam began to speak, but George cut him short. *"No – it's alright – she's changed her mind – but it will be up to you to make sure he doesn't cause any problems. If he's yours, you will be responsible for him – whatever he does – but I'll always help if I can."*

Not for the first time since he had come home from hospital Sam felt grateful to George. His *"Thank you,"* was sincere.

George nodded. *"We're nearly there. Give them a call Sam – say we'll be ten minutes."*

Clive Baker was in his office with Ben at his feet under the desk.

"Come on out old dog and listen to me," said Clive. *"This is an important day for you."*

Shaking himself, as dogs do, Ben emerged and sat looking up at Clive.

"Ben," he began. *"The boy Sam will be here soon and I ..."*

He stopped in mid-sentence as his secretary, Jean came in.

"Clive, the boy just 'phoned..." She stopped. *"Clive, I worry about you and that dog. You talk to him as though he was another human being. I've said it before, but it's true. I have never known you like that with another dog."*

Ben dropped his head to avoid meeting her eyes.

Clive got up, raised a hand to Ben, saying, *"Stay Dog Stay,"* and ushering her out of the room, followed into her office, closing the door behind him.

Clive shuffled awkwardly, which was entirely unlike his normal way and still seemed hesitant as he spoke.

"Jean – in some ways I would love to keep that dog. In others I'll be glad to see the back of him." Jean looked at him, as she spoke.

"Yes, there is something odd about him. In fact, almost everything about him is odd. Why did someone put your name on his dog tag? As for that 'phone call from the old lady – what did she say? That Ben had come from Russia to find you and that if you thought that unlikely, it would get even more unlikely."

She shook her head. *"I know what you mean. So does Steve. He said that he did not have to show Ben what to do – he could just tell him and Ben would do it. But you have made up your mind to let him go to the boy haven't you?"*

Clive thought for a moment, then pulled himself together.

"Yes – I have. We settled that the other day and the boy will be here any minute. If they get on, that's it. If not – I just don't know what to do. But whoever sent him here wanted him to be a help dog."

"Hmm," said Jean. *"Unless he just decided for himself."*

The sound of George's car on the gravel outside jolted them both out of their uncertain mood. Clive retreated rapidly into his office telling Jean to bring the boy in to see him.

Ben was feeling as uncertain as Clive. Like any dog, what he wanted most was a faithful master, a dry warm bed, enough to eat and plenty of exercise and fun – but he knew he was much more than just any old dog.

He quite liked Clive, but he did not want to be just a dog helping train other dogs and he did not want to share his master with all the other dogs at Canine Partners.

Nor did he want to be handed over to the police or the military – or kept to help Steve Judge to train other dogs. Boris said he should become a help dog and that was what he would be. Anyway, no dog can have two masters and Ben needed a human he could trust and be with all his life, just as much as the boy Sam needed a friend whom he could trust to be a friend always. He hated the uncertainty and he just wished he could be back at home with Boris. Clive's voice broke into his thoughts.

"Ben – what's wrong – you look sad?"

For a moment, Ben almost told him of all his worries and fears – then thought better of it. He simply got up, looked at Clive's face and gave a soft whimper before settling down again, head on paws, under the desk.

He heard voices in Jean's office, her knock on the door and Clive's command, *"Come in."* Ben kept his head down and waited as Sam and George met Clive. George was thanking Clive, but Sam was looking hard at Ben.

"Is that Ben?" he asked.

Clive smiled at him. *"Yes, I'll introduce him. Come on Ben. This is Sam. He needs a friend – a dog friend – a canine partner – you see, he can't walk or stand."*

The dog came and sat by the chair.

Very quietly, Clive told Sam, *"Just say knee."*

Sam obeyed. Ben laid his chin on the boy's knee.

"Now say, my lap." Again Sam repeated the command and Ben put his front paws on the boy's lap.

"Well, that's a start," said Clive. *"Now, tell him to sit and if you're ready, take him out and have a look round. He'll guide you to meet Steve, our trainer. All you do is say, Lets go, and he'll stick to you like treacle to a blanket."*

Sam could hardly speak – except to say, *"Thank you, Mr Baker,"* before he was out of the office, past Jean's desk and with Ben opening the doors for him, they were off across the grass to the training centre.

The two men watched from the window, laughing at the boy and the dog.

"I think it might work," said Clive. *"We have never given a dog to anyone as young as Sam before, but Ben is such an unusual one – and he is older than most of ours, but he will need a bit more training. Now, tell me – what is it like for the boy at home and at school? Shah told me he was with his father when they had the crash. It must be difficult for you to replace his father."*

"I couldn't," said George. *"And I don't try. His mother and father's marriage broke up – I suppose that was partly my fault. Anyway, she came to live with me and brought the children. I'm afraid Sam can't forgive me for that. So I don't try to be his father. I'm better at being a sort of elder brother or friend – and saving him and his mother from falling out. Shah was right. He needs a friend always loyal to him. Now what happens next?"*

Clive explained that the boy and the dog would do some training together.

Usually, that would last weeks, but if they liked each other and got on, as Ben was so quick to learn, it could be cut to a few days.

"We're cutting a lot of corners," he told George. "But I think Ben needs a new master as much as Sam needs a dog. He is not like any other dog I have ever known. His ability to understand humans is far, far beyond normal."

In a few moments Clive recounted the story of Ben's mysterious arrival at the Exeter police station as a stray, but with a clean, bright new tag with his own name and that of Clive Baker on it. Then, looking very hard at George, he continued, "I'm prepared to take a risk and let him go to Sam – provided you think Sam is willing to learn how to manage a dog – and provided you and his mother are prepared to do your bit and make a home for a quite exceptional animal."

George thought for a moment, looked out of the window to see Sam and Ben and the trainer, Steve, then turned back to Clive.

"I think it will work. Of course, Sam hasn't got over losing his father. He doesn't get on with his mother, although he is okay with his sister and she could help with the dog. But he needs to get away from the past – he spends too much time thinking about what might have been. The dog will help him build a new life."

Clive nodded, picked up the papers on his desk and handed them to George.

"Okay – let's go for it. Take these through to Jean and she'll start fixing everything. Just let me know if there are any problems."

Within an hour Sam and George were on their way home, Sam bubbling over with excitement, telling George that Ben understood everything said to him and that he didn't need any more training.

"Why can't he come home with me now?" Sam asked.

George smiled. "Sam," he said. "It may be you – and your mother – who need some training more than he does, but it won't be long."

Nor was it very long. It was the half term holiday the following week and Sam spent the days at Canine Partners working with Ben, Steve and the other trainers, dogs and disabled people. On the second day George pretended he had to go to London and persuaded Sam's mother to take him to his training session. He telephoned Steve, the trainer, to ask him to explain to her what

Ben would do for Sam, and what he would need by way of his bed and board.

Sam's mother was not best pleased at having to spend her day at a school for dogs, grumbling about dogs wasting her time. Sam realised he had come to get on far better with George than with his own mother, but thought it best to say nothing. Steve, the trainer, pretended he knew nothing about all that and invited Sam's mother to come into one of the training sessions with some of the dogs and their prospective owners – or partners, as Steve and Clive Baker always called them.

Sam greeted Ben as though they were the oldest of friends. He had really fallen for Ben even before he had seen him. The boy had lost his father – who had been his best friend. People – all of them, except his sister, Sophie and perhaps George – had let him down and he needed and wanted a true and loyal friend.

Ben was much more cautious. Although he, too, had lost his best ever friend Boris, Boris' warnings to be careful about who he should trust stuck in his mind. He knew he had been almost reckless in talking to the man, John at Teignmouth, the little old lady, Alice Hanson and Clive Baker too. He was determined not to run the risk of just being used by the police – or the military – or even Clive Baker, or becoming some sort of freak dog in a circus. He liked Sam and realised that they had both lost their best friends, but he could see that living with Sam would be very different to his life with Boris.

Other humans respected Boris. He had been their pack leader. Boris said what should be done and other humans did as he asked. In fact, he was rather like Clive Baker. But Sam was only a boy – just a pup and in many ways, thought Ben, he, not Sam, would be the leader. Or perhaps Steve was right, he and Sam would be partners.

Dogs don't usually think or feel like that. Although they have lived with humans for tens of thousands of years, they are still pack animals like wolves at heart, and if every human in the world vanished without a trace one night, their dogs would soon gang up into packs and every pack would have its leader. And, thought Ben (and quite rightly) humans are pack animals too.

Sam's voice cut into Ben's thoughts.

"Come on Ben – what are you dreaming about? Wake up. I said my lap."

Ben shook himself and almost said sorry – but managed to stop himself just in time, and put his front paws into the boy's lap.

Sam told him he was a good dog and slipped him a doggie treat from his bag of tiny pieces of biscuit, carrot and dried meat.

"Look, look," said Sam, staring hard at a ball on the floor at the other side of the room. Ben turned to follow Sam's gaze. *"Get it,"* commanded Sam, and Ben, quite enjoying the game, was off like a shot to retrieve and then on the command, *"Bring it here,"* to take the ball back to the boy.

One routine followed another, the boy laughing and the dog tail wagging as they enjoyed the fun.

Like a good head trainer, Steve was watching, correcting and encouraging all his pupils, humans and canines alike, but he was also watching Sam's mother. Her body language was changing. She was no longer stiff and scarcely suppressing her bad temper. She too, was watching, listening and although she said nothing, her lips were beginning to move as she began in her mind to encourage her son and the dog.

Although she was actually speaking in her mind and not saying the word out loud, Ben could still hear her. He waited for the right moment and when Sam was looking at Steve, he moved quickly across to Sam's mother, sat in front of her, licked her hand and was back beside Sam's chair before the boy had missed him.

As they drove home, it was Sam's mother who spoke first. *"Sam – that dog – he is a bit unusual isn't he?"*

"Well, not really," the boy replied. *"They are all being trained to help their masters or mistresses."*

"No," she continued. *"I didn't mean that. It was almost as though he knew what I was thinking. You didn't see, but he came over to me – just to sort of say, hello, and was back beside you before you knew he had gone..."*

Sam interrupted her. *"Oh, they all say that about him. He can pick up what you are feeling or saying before you really quite know yourself. I hope you will like him. I'm sure he will be very good."*

She looked round at the boy and to his surprise said, *"I think he will be good for all of us."*

They both fell silent – hoping that would be so.

It was Sam who broke the long silence.

"Thank you Mum. Thank you for understanding."

She turned to look at him, taking her eyes off the road for a moment.

"No, thank you, Sam."

Sam had not felt so close to his mother since the awful day she had left his father to live with George. That night he slept better than he had for months.

On Thursday, George had dropped Sam at Canine Partners for another day of training and when he arrived to pick him up that evening, Clive Baker was waiting for him. He handed George a note and Sam noticed that as he read it, George began to smile.

"What does it say?" Sam asked. George's smile became wider.

"It seems that you and Ben have passed all your tests. If your mother comes with you tomorrow, you can take him home – provided we have got everything he needs – like a bed and food."

For a minute, Sam could hardly speak.

"Thank you. Thank you Mr Baker," he stammered. *"Does Ben know?"*

Clive took the boy by the arm, gave George a nod and said, *"Let's tell him the news."*

CHAPTER EIGHT

BEN JOINS SAM

Sam's mother, to his great relief, seemed pleased when he told her that evening. Then, as mothers do, she began to organise things ready for Ben. Sam had been afraid she really did not want him to have a dog, but she seemed happy enough even suggesting (to Sam's delight) that Ben should sleep in his room.

"But, not on your bed. We'll get him one of his own tomorrow morning. And you, Sam, will be responsible for feeding him and taking him for walks. And if he makes a mess – you will have to clear it up – even if you are in a wheelchair."

Sam was almost too happy to hear what she was saying. He hardly noticed what he was eating for dinner or what was on the TV for thinking about bringing Ben home. He was up early next morning waiting for George to take him to the pet shop to buy everything Ben would need before going to fetch him from Canine Partners.

Being a Labrador, Ben ate his dinner as usual and had no trouble in falling asleep. Although his dreams were about Boris and his life in Russia, once he was awake, Ben began to think about his new life. Most important of all, Clive Baker had not told anyone his secret. Should he tell Sam? He really would have to, but suppose Sam told other people? What then?

It was all rather difficult, so Ben did what dogs are good at doing. He simply put it to the back of his mind and thought about breakfast instead. So much had happened since Boris had told him he had to come to England less than a month ago and despite his worries, Ben just hoped that after all his adventures life would settle down.

Whenever he did think about his journey, he thought most of all about the little old lady, Alice Hanson. It was she who had helped him when he had felt really alone and lost. It was odd, he often thought, but she was a bit like Boris. She had an air of authority about her and people did what she said.

Strangely enough, although Ben could not have known, the little old lady, Alice Hanson, had been thinking about him too. It was more than two weeks since she had found him – or perhaps since he had found her. She knew that Clive had picked up Ben from the police station in Exeter because she had 'phoned to find out what had become of him, but as the days had gone by, she had been thinking more and more about Ben.

Next morning Ben was up early exploring his new home. Sam was happier than he had been since the crash which had killed his father and left him unable to walk. Sam's mother seemed pleased to see him happy. So were George and Sam's sister, Sophie. She thought Ben was great and had to be told he was not a family pet, but Sam's working help dog.

Ben thought the house was a bit dull. It was quite large with a big garden. There were not many interesting smells – except in the kitchen of course. There was the scent of a cat in the garden and that was about it. He liked Sam's room which had been George's office, and now had a bathroom built onto it. It was quite big with two big chairs as well as Sam's bed and a desk, bookcases and cupboards. There was plenty of room for his bed, which was near the radiator, and there was a water bowl under the desk.

Sam had watched as Ben made his reconnaissance of the house and garden, cataloguing in his mind all the scents, the best of all in the kitchen of course, and he caught the smell of a bottle of whisky – the same sort that both his Master Boris and Clive Baker drank – in a cupboard in the sitting room, then came back and sat beside his wheelchair. Ben still felt homesick when he thought of Boris and his home in Russia – but somehow the thought that

Boris, George and Clive Baker – all liked the same drink was reassuring.

Over the weekend Ben learned the routine of Sam's life. He could help him put on and take off his clothes. He opened doors; picked up things from the floor (and like all teenage boys, Sam's things had a habit of finding themselves on the floor). He helped Sam move from the wheelchair to his bed. Best of all, he ran alongside Sam when they were out together and helped push and pull the wheelchair up kerbs or through soft patches of ground in the park and the woods where they went to play. The woods and the park were absolutely full of all manner of scents – of other dogs – and strange ones he had never smelled before – foxes and badgers, a bit like dog, but quite distinct. He almost asked Sam what they were – but, of course, the boy wouldn't know, he thought. And there were birds and little things like mice and, of course, rabbits and even stoats and weasels.

At times, it was all too much for him and he quite forgot poor Sam, coming back shamefaced when Sam whistled.

Listening to Sam's mother and George from under the table, Ben realised the next week would be different. School would start again on Tuesday and he would have to look after Sam – even warning other boys if they pushed or jostled him. But something was being planned for Monday. Ben longed to simply ask about it, but he was determined not to reveal his secret to anyone else except Sam – and he still worried that Sam might blurt it out to other people, so he stayed quiet. He was, thought Ben, only a pup really.

At last he worked it out. George was going to take Sam to his father's flat. The police would be there to meet them to help because they knew that someone had been in the flat and taken Sam's father's computer and searched the flat as though they were looking for something.

CHAPTER NINE

BEN VISITS HIS FATHER'S FLAT
– ALICE GOES TO TRING

As Ben and Sam were getting up on Monday morning to go to Sam's father's flat, Alice Hanson was already up drinking her first cup of tea, wondering if she should telephone Clive Baker to enquire about Ben. She tried to forget about it and get on with her breakfast, but it was no good. Eventually, she pushed aside her breakfast toast and folded shut her newspaper. She was irritated with herself. It was less than three weeks, she told herself, since she had taken the lost Labrador dog, Ben, to the police station in Exeter. She knew that Clive Baker had collected him because the police had told her so when she enquired. But what had happened since?

It was no good – her curiosity was getting the better of her. She knew that she had not imagined it all. Well, she really couldn't have done, could she – she thought. But every now and again she had begun to doubt herself. After all, dogs can't talk – but then, Ben had talked to her.

She just had to know. The question was how to find out without making a fool of herself. However, she looked at it, the answer was always the same.

Her only contact with Ben was through Clive Baker at Canine Partners, so somehow without looking plain silly, she would have to 'phone him and ask after the dog.

She hesitated time and time again. She half read the morning paper – hesitated again, then pulled herself together. *"Come on,"* she thought. *"Come on – it is going 9.30 am, so Clive Baker will be in his office. The number is still on my mobile 'phone – I'll give him a call."*

Moments later the 'phone rang on Clive Baker's desk.

"It's the old lady," Clive's secretary, Jean, told him. *"The one who rang about Ben. Do you remember?"*

Clive groaned. *"Not her – the one who said the police would ring. What does she want?"*

"Just to ask if Ben is alright I think," said Jean. *"Shall I put her through?"*

Clive took a deep breath. *"Alright – I can't really avoid talking to her, can I?"*

In a moment Miss Hanson was through to him.

"Good morning Mr Baker. I'm sorry to trouble you, but I am the lady who took Ben into the police station at Exeter and I was just wondering how he has been getting on?"

"Yes, I remember," replied Clive. *"You told me he was a remarkable dog – and that was certainly right. I've never known a dog learn so much so quickly as he has. He is an absolute star, isn't he?"*

Alice realised that either Ben had not told Clive his secret – or if he had, Clive was not giving much away. Hasn't Ben told him, she wondered, or is he fishing to find out what I know? She ignored Clive's question and asked one of her own instead.

"Have you found him a home yet?"

"Yes, he is looking after a boy of 14. He broke his back in a car crash which killed his father, so he needed a good friend. I think they are both getting on very well."

All Alice Hanson's training and experience in the murky world of spies and intelligence work came to her aid. In a few minutes she had wormed out of Clive Baker, the boy's name, where he lived, how he had been injured and his father killed, and where he went to school, before he realised she had told him absolutely nothing in return;

"Thank you so much, Mr Baker. I'm so glad to know Ben is okay. Goodbye."
And she was gone.

Jean opened the office door and looked enquiringly at him.

"Bloody hell!" he barked. *"Bloody hell! That old girl is as smart as that dog. She gives nothing away and I just wonder if Ben was telling the truth and ..."* His voice died away as he realised his secretary was looking very intently at him.

"I mean, well I mean – oh, bloody hell – I think I ought to go and look to see what everyone is doing."

Jean stood aside to let him go by and stared after him as he marched across the yard.

"That dog," she said, *"has done more to unsettle him than the IRA, the Serbs, Albanians, Iraqis and all the others he tangled with in his life as a Royal Marine commando."*

Meanwhile, Alice Hanson had been looking at her road atlas. Although she really did not like driving far any more, there was really no sensible alternative. She did not really like computers very much either – but, she thought, they had their uses. In a few moments she had Googled 'Tring', printed out a map of the town, found the school, looked at it on Google Earth, and printed out the route instructions for the drive from Exeter.

"Tring – Tring," she muttered to herself. *"Why do I know the name of that place?"*

Suddenly, it came back to her. Jack Riley – one of her oldest friends from her days in MI6 had bought a house near Tring a year earlier and in his card last Christmas, had invited her to stay there.

For an elderly lady, Alice Hanson moved very quickly once she had made up her mind. Within minutes she had telephoned her old friend to ask if she could stay with him for a few days. In no time at all she had packed her bag and was heading up the M5 towards Tring.

Once Alice Hanson had arrived at Jack Riley's house and unpacked her bag, she explained that she "had to go on a little reconnaissance." She soon found Sam's school and waited to follow the boy and the dog on their way home and into the park.

They were so concerned with each other that neither Sam nor Ben noticed the little old lady watching them in the park. She wore dark clothing and stood very still, just in front of the dark trunk of a big oak tree so she was not easy to see. She had also positioned herself downwind from the boy and the dog so her scent would not carry on the wind to Ben's sensitive nose. She waited until Sam and Ben were well out of the park and on their way home before making her way back to the car. Then with the windows closed, her hat pulled well down and her coat collar well up, she drove very slowly at a safe distance behind them until she saw them at their front door.

That evening over dinner at Jack Riley's house, Alice Hanson talked a lot about their days working for the secret intelligence service. Eventually Jack turned the conversation to the reason for her visit to Tring.

"Alice," he queried. *"Just why are you so interested in this boy and the dog?"*
Alice thought carefully before she replied.

"Well Jack. Somewhere I can smell an interesting story. I gather the boy's father was killed in an unexplained car crash – and the boy was left paralysed from his waist down. The father was a journalist who was on the track of a really big drug racket. The dog – well, I'll tell you more about him later. But right now, he is the boy's care dog – they call them canine partners."

"Ah," said Jack. *"I can tell you a bit about the boy's father. He was Charles Turner, a local chap. There was often something about him in the local press – although mostly in recent times they were sad stories. His wife left him for a boring local teacher and then, of course, the car smash that killed him."*

Alice drew a deep breath.

"Then I had better find out a bit more tomorrow. Perhaps I should look at those stories in the local paper. In the meantime, I'm tired already and tomorrow might be a busy day. I think I'll head off to bed."

Sam, Sophie, George and Ben had set off quite early that morning as the flat was in London's Docklands, quite near to the Thames. Sam's mother said she did not want to go with them, so it was just his sister Sophie and George, and, of course, Ben – who made the trip to London. George was right. There were two CID police detectives waiting for them. Sophie and Sam found it all very hard. The last time they had been in the flat, it was with their father. It had felt warm and lived in, and they had made some tea and had laughed and joked. He had told them that he had infiltrated one of the biggest drug smuggling and dealing gangs in the country.

"*Before long,*" he had told them, "*I'll take all my information to the police. I've been working for the gang for months now and I've got them all – even the bosses – on film and audio tapes. I have to be careful – they wouldn't be very pleased if they knew. And it will make a terrific TV documentary. No-one has ever done anything half as good before.*"

Sophie had told him to be careful. "*Dad, do you have to do this sort of thing?*" she had asked him.

"*Yes, for two reasons,*" he had answered. "*First, it's my job. I'm a TV crime reporter. Second, I hate these people. They push drugs that wreck people's lives. They push addicts into crime to make the money to buy the drugs and sooner or later the drugs rot their minds and bodies. Then they leave them to die on the streets or in some filthy squat – or even in prison. All of the drug smugglers, dealers and the gang bosses need to be in jail – especially the bosses. No-one suspects them. They live in big houses, send their kids to good schools – they even give money to charities. People would never believe where that money comes from.*"

Sophie and Sam wondered if the drugs gang would ever be caught now. Then Sam realised why the flat had been burgled. It must have been the drugs gang. They must have suspected his father knew too much. It must have been the gang looking for the files and tapes containing the evidence his father had gathered.

George's voice broke into his thoughts. "*Sam, are you alright?*" He realised that Ben was looking at him too. He was gripping the wheels of his chair so tightly that his knuckles were white.

"*I'm sorry,*" said Sam. "*I was just upset – I'm alright now.*"

"*Then shall we look at anything you and Sophie would like to take? Your mother says she doesn't want anything and asked me to give anything you don't want to a charity shop.*"

Ben had the deep furrow running across his head, from just between his eyes to past his ears. It always showed up like a human's frown when he was thinking hard. He got up quietly and began to pace around the room. He sniffed carefully at the two policemen who, of course, could not read Sam's thoughts as Ben had done. He could pick up the scent of a man – a bit like Sam's scent. Then he went into the bedroom where it was very strong and he knew it must be the scent of Sam's father. Then back into the living room past the bookcases and the music tapes, and the chairs, into the office and over the files and tapes on the floor, all the time picking up scents and filing them away in his brain as dogs do – just like humans, remembering images of things and people they have seen. He had no problem identifying the scent of Sam and Sophie's father. To a dog, we have a family scent – just the way humans notice that we may look like our parents, siblings or even cousins. But here were some other scents too. Quite new. Some of them only weeks old – of people who had not been in the flat more than once – or twice at the most. He could tell that the two policemen had been there once before – but so had two other people, and one of them smelt of something Boris had called "drugs".

He came back to Sam's side, watching and listening as the boy and his sister began to look through the tapes. Sam had inherited his father's love of classical music, but Sophie preferred modern pop, so they divided the music tapes, old videos and CDs. As for the books, Sophie took those on arts and the novels, and Sam cornered those on cars, sports and the old history books.

The detectives did not seem to do much. They just sat or stood around and talked quietly, giving Ben a gentle pat as he went and sat near them. Of course they did not know how much more he knew about who had been in the flat, than they, George, Sam or Sophie could know.

Nor did they know that Ben was listening to what they were saying.

"It is odd," one said. *"Whoever came in here either had a key or was very good at picking the locks without making a mess. It was a very professional job. It wasn't some junkie looking for cash or something to sell for cash to buy drugs."*

"Yes," agreed the other detective. *"It wasn't an ordinary break-in. Whoever it was, was looking for something particular and wasn't interested in anything else. But what was it and did he find it?"*

The first detective looked very thoughtful. *"You don't think the boy's father was in some way mixed up with the people who broke in? Were they all in some crooked business? There is something we don't know and I don't think we ever will know either."*

Ben did not really understand much of this, but he knew well enough that the police thought there was something more to it than just an ordinary break-in. Sam was beginning to wonder about it all too and when Ben went back to sit by his wheelchair he put a hand down and rubbed the dog's head.

"There's something that doesn't make sense about all this, old dog." He said. *"But we won't work it out tonight, so we had better be heading back home."* George and Sophie thought so too. With the help of the detectives, they got Sam back to the car and headed for home.

CHAPTER TEN

BEN TELLS SAM HIS SECRET

Ben slept badly that Monday night. That would be bad enough for a human, but for a Labrador dog, it was almost frightening. When he did drop off he dreamed – mostly about his life in Russia with Boris. When he was awake he did not worry – dogs do not worry like humans – but he felt very insecure about his new life in England. It was so different. Boris was a pack leader. Other humans did what he told them. There was usually no-one else except Boris' man, Nikita, in the house and mostly Ben and Boris talked to each other, just like two humans. Sometimes Boris went skiing and Ben rushed after him sliding down the snow. It was such fun.

Now it was all so different. They would be going to school in the morning – but what would that be like? The training school at Canine Partners had been fun – but what would he have to do when he went to school with Sam?

Ben felt very insecure and lonely. What he did not quite understand was that he was indeed not like other people's dogs. He needed more from his master than just a warm, dry bed, food and a water bowl. He – just like Sam – needed a real friend. Eventually the worries and thoughts stopped going round and round and, as a Labrador should, he fell peacefully asleep.

The alarm clock woke him. It was Tuesday morning. Sam was calling to him.

"Ben – fetch my wheelchair."

Ben was out of bed in a moment and pushing at the wheelchair to get it alongside Sam's bed.

"My legs," commanded Sam. In an instant Ben was on his hind legs nosing his head and paws under Sam's paralysed legs and dragging them over the edge of his bed.

Sam held out a rope handle.

"Tug, tug," he ordered, and with a heave from Ben, Sam was sitting on the edge of his bed. With a shuffle he was off the bed, into his wheelchair and heading for the bathroom.

"Look, look," said Sam, staring at the rope handle on the bathroom door.

"Tug, tug." Ben pulled the door open. To Ben it was all a great game – and, of course, all help dogs are taught to understand those sort of commands. For Ben it was much easier because although he had not told Sam his secret. Sam realised that Ben seemed to understand everything he said and, more strangely sometimes, what he had really only thought of saying.

It didn't take Sam long to get up. A quick shower (and how Ben wished he was allowed to shower too) and he was back in the bedroom with Ben opening drawers and handing him his clothes. Then out to the kitchen and a quick visit to the garden for Ben before breakfast.

It wasn't far to school – only about twenty minutes walk – and Sam had learned to propel his wheelchair at quite a speed with Ben trotting along beside him, except when it needed an extra push or pull up and down kerbs or slopes.

As they approached the school the footpath became full of teenage boys and girls, all talking and shouting. Ben noticed Sam's sister, Sophie with a group of older girls and boys, but somehow managing to keep an eye on her brother. Some of Sam's friends came to walk with him, all talking and shouting, some wanted to talk to Ben. But Ben was wearing his work jacket – bright yellow with black lettering saying, *"CANINE PARTNERS – I am a working dog. Please do not distract me."*

Boys, being boys, (and the girls were nearly as bad), they wanted to say hello to Ben and some – despite Sam telling them not to – wanted to offer him sweets or sandwiches – or even chocolate, although chocolate, except the special stuff for dogs, is poisonous to them.

It was hard going for Sam and Ben too. They were both relieved when the doors opened and the pupils went flooding in. There was a ramp for Sam and the headmaster, old "Stuffy" Brown, was there ready to welcome Ben with a cheerful shout of "*Good dog. Good dog. Now give Sam and his dog a bit of room.*" Not that Ben, who was a pretty big Labrador, was above a bit of pushing and shoving himself if he thought anyone might tread on his paws. The corridor to Sam's classroom was quite one of the noisiest places he had ever been in. There was so much shouting and talking that he could hardly pick out what Sam was saying.

Eventually Sam found his place. It was fairly obvious really. There was no chair and the desk had been cut to let Sam get his knees underneath more easily. Suddenly a voice, not that loud, but very clear, rang out.

"*Quiet. Quiet.*"

It came from a very small woman, who in traditional style wore a black gown over her dark dress. The room fell silent.

"*Wow!*" thought Ben. "*That is a real pack leader.*"

"*Good morning,*" she continued and pausing only for the class to reply, "*Good morning Miss Scott,*" went on.

"*It's nice to see you all back after half term – and with one extra pupil too. Welcome Ben. I hope you - and Sam – will let us know if you are comfortable.*"

Ben almost said, "*Good morning, Miss Scott,*" but stopped himself just in time – but he stood up and wagged his tail.

Miss Scott stared hard at him – then at Sam – as she asked Sam,

"*Sam, does your dog understand everything people say to him? I'm sure he knew what I said just then.*"

"*Well Miss,*" said Sam. "*He does seem to understand quite a lot.*"

Miss Scott thought for a moment and almost questioned Sam again, but Sam spoke first.

"*Thank you Miss. I think Ben will be quite happy curled up somewhere until break time when I'll take him out.*" And Ben did curl up under the desk – but he kept a wary eye on Miss Scott.

With the register marked, the school day began. Ben soon opted out of maths – dogs are not very good at counting more than five of anything – after that it is lots, or lots and lots. Nor did he really take much interest at first in most other lessons, although the rabbits in the biology laboratory had him sniffing the air and wagging his tail, but mostly the day was a bit boring except when a couple of rather foolish boys threatened to push Sam about. Ben quite enjoyed being told to see them off.

Although Sam was the only badly disabled pupil at Tring School, it had all the things like ramps and a toilet with extra space and a seat higher than normal to be level with the seat of his wheelchair. There was a lot of laughing from the other boys when they realised that Ben helped Sam even there. Sam thought how much harder it would have been without Ben whilst Ben rather enjoyed that fact this his master was someone special.

The day passed quickly enough, although by 3.30 pm, Ben was looking forward to getting home to his dinner. Except for when he was asleep, Ben had watched Sam even more closely than Sam had watched him. Ben began to realise that Sam's sister, Sophie was never too far away to help if help was needed.

Ben decided that although it was not all that different to his life in Russia before Boris became too ill to go to work, he did miss the talks they used to have when no-one could hear them. Ben decided he would have to tell Sam of his secret before long. But, when he wondered?

As in life, questions like that often answer themselves. On the way home from school Sam was whizzing along quite fast and because of a high hedge, just did not see a car backing out of a drive. Ben heard it too late to get in front of the wheelchair to warn Sam of the danger. Without thinking he shouted, *"Stop – Sam – Stop,"* and grabbed the sleeve of Sam's jacket. They stopped just in time as the car backed across the footpath into the road and drove off.

"Whew – that was close – thank you Ben," Sam said without thinking – and then, *"Ben – Ben – Am I going crazy or did you shout, 'Stop' at me?"*

Ben looked round. There was no-one else in sight except Sophie and she was a good hundred yards away.

Ben put his paws up on Sam's knees and looked, as he always did when he wanted to say something important to humans, straight into the boy's eyes.

"Master," he said. *"Master – yes – I did say 'Stop'. And you heard me in your head just as you hear me now. And when you speak – even if it is very quietly – just inside your head, I can hear you in my head and understand what you say."*

Sam simply stared at the dog. He was too stunned to speak out loud, just muttering to himself. *"I must be going mad. Dogs can't talk."*

"No, Master," Ben whispered to him. *"No. I cannot talk like people talk, but you can hear me in your head and I can hear you in mine."*

"Why didn't you tell me before? Who else knows about this? Does Clive Baker know? Ben – am I dreaming?"

"No Master. You are not dreaming. No-one else around here knows. It is my secret and Boris, my old master, told me not to let anyone know unless I had to do so and unless I trusted them. Master – you won't tell anyone else? Please don't. If other people knew, I really don't know what would happen to me. You are my master – and I will look after you – but please, Master – you must look after me."

Sam looked quite white and shocked. Then he heard his sister, Sophie calling out to him.

"Sam. Are you alright? I thought that car was going to hit you."

Ben dropped back down onto his four feet, but kept staring hard at Sam, who turned in his chair as Sophie caught up with them.

"Yes. Yes. I'm okay. Ben must have heard the car, although we couldn't see it because of the hedge and he grabbed my sleeve. I think I'd better take him into the park to give him a run to say thank you."

Brother and sister and Ben together, continued along the path to the park gates and then, telling Sophie to let their mother know he was giving Ben an extra run, Sam turned into the park.

There were not many people there and within moments they found a quiet corner where Ben nipped in front of the wheelchair, went down on his belly with his forelegs stretched out in front of him looking at Sam as he had been taught to do if he wanted to get his master's attention.

"Thank you Master, for not telling Sophie."

Sam still looked shattered – as though he was still doubting his own mind.

"Ben," he said. *"I must be dreaming – I really must – or I'm going crazy..."*

The dog interrupted his words by standing up again on his hind legs with his front paws on the boy's lap and giving him a great big lick.

"*Master – it is a long story and I will tell you everything tonight when everyone has gone to bed and the house is quiet. For now I will just tell you I am not an ordinary dog – but a dog who can hear in my head the signals that your brain or anyone else's brain makes as you speak. And I can make those signals so strongly in my head that you – or anyone else – can hear me in theirs.*"

"But Ben – why did you go to the Canine Partners school? Why did you leave your master?"

Ben's eyes dropped, his ears flopped down and his head fell into Sam's lap.

"*My master, Boris was very ill. I think he is now dead. We lived in a place called Serov and he said it would not be safe to stay in Russia without him, so he sent me to Canine Partners.*"

"You came from Russia? This gets crazier every minute", interrupted Sam.

"*No Master – I do not understand all these things – but it is true. Now please Master – I am hungry and I would like a bonio before my dinner and it is getting cold here, and I think it will start to rain before long – I can smell the rain in the air – please can we go home and <u>please</u> don't tell anyone about this and I will tell you everything tonight when everyone is asleep.*"

Sam drew a deep breath.

"Okay Ben – but I still think I might be dreaming."

Ben looked at him, gave a little bark and then said very gently, "*I'll say nothing more until everyone is in bed – but remember I can hear what you say.*"

They turned and with Ben trotting alongside the wheelchair resumed the journey home.

At home that evening Sam could hardly conceal his impatience to have dinner and get to bed. His mother noticed that he seemed not quite himself and as she was setting the table for breakfast, George noticed that she kept putting things down and picking them up again.

"What's wrong?" he eventually asked her. "Are you worried about something?"

"Well, not really," she replied, "but didn't you think Sam was acting a bit strangely this evening? He hardly said a word at dinner, then just went straight to bed. It isn't like him."

George thought before answering her. "*Yes, I did. And he didn't say anything about the prizes he is going to get at his school prizegiving day tomorrow. I am sure they must have told him about it. It is a copy of his father's book about the way the big drug dealers have bought proper businesses to conceal their drug smuggling. Perhaps it all reminded him of the car crash that killed his father.*"

"*Perhaps so,*" she said. "*It is just as well he's got that dog – he's a real friend.*"

And like a really good friend, Ben was helping Sam get to bed, then in the very softest whisper telling him that he would wait until everyone else was in bed before he began to tell Sam the story of how he came from Russia to Canine Partners.

Dogs are more patient than teenage boys and Ben found it easy enough to wait until his ears told him that everyone else was asleep. Then, tucking his nose under Sam's duvet to make sure he was awake, he said very quietly,

"*Master, what I am going to tell you is a secret not many people know. Just my old master Boris, his man Nikita, the man I found in Teignmouth, a little old lady and Clive Baker, the man at Canine Partners.*"

"*That,*" said Sam very wisely, "*is quite a lot to keep a secret.*"

Ben agreed, then went on to tell Sam his story. The boy hardly interrupted him at all, listening intently to every word.

It was just gone midnight when Ben finished saying, "*And now Master, I am your dog, your canine partner.*"

Sam hardly knew what to say. It was hard to believe that he had a dog he could talk to or who could talk to him. He kept asking himself if it were all a dream – and when he did, he heard Ben saying to him, "*No Master, I am real and we can talk to each other.*"

Sam scratched Ben's ears – the way dogs like humans to, saying,

"*It will be a busy day tomorrow old dog – we had best get some rest.*"

And in moments they were both sound asleep.

CHAPTER ELEVEN

DETECTIVE WORK

Whilst Sam had been getting ready for his first day at school with Ben, Alice Hanson was busy at her detective work. At breakfast she had asked her old friend, John Riley, for directions to the offices of the local newspaper, *The Tring Advertiser*. Not only did he know just where the office was, but he knew the editor quite well and in no time at all he had made a 'phone call to arrange for Alice Hanson to search through all their reports on Sam's father, particularly those on the car crash in which Sam had been injured and his father killed.

There were accounts going back over several years of TV programmes and national newspaper stories of Sam's father, Charles Turner's investigations into big City frauds, corrupt police officers, smuggling and all sorts of rackets. Alice Hanson noticed that more recently, the reports were more about Sam's father's campaign to track down the people running the drugs trade. Then she found a report of the death of Sam's uncle – his father's brother. He had started taking cannabis while he was still at school and had a long string of convictions for minor drug offences before getting hooked on cocaine.

Alice Hanson read in the report on the inquest into his death that no-one could be sure if he had died of an overdose of cocaine or had been murdered in a row with a drug dealer. *"That,"* she thought, *"explains a lot,"* as she turned back to the papers reporting the crash in which Sam's father had been killed. The inquest had been very short and concluded that it was most likely he had fallen asleep and driven off the road, down a steep bank into a large tree. No witnesses to the actual crash had come forward. A police officer reported that Sam, who was still in hospital at the time, could not remember anything at all about the accident. A lorry driver told the inquest that he had been overtaken by two cars driving quite close together just before the crash and that was all. Alice Hanson's life in the intelligence service had made her suspicious of fatal accidents without any witnesses, to people who knew too much for their own good.

"I wonder – I wonder," she said to herself.

Had Sam's father discovered too much for his own good about one of the really big drug smuggling and selling gangs? If he had, they would have had no hesitation in "arranging an accident". She sat looking at the pages of the old newspapers. Suddenly, she flashed back through the pages to the report of the crash.

There it was. Charles Turner had taken Sam to the cinema to see a film. They had met in town, had a pizza at about 7 pm, going to the cinema at about 8 pm and left London around 10.30 pm. There was no reason to think he was tired – he had not had a drink – the medical report at the inquest said there was no alcohol in his blood. He would have been talking to Sam about the film and what Sam had been doing since they last saw each other. Why should Sam's father have fallen asleep? And what about that other car? Suppose – suppose ...

Alice Hanson shook her head. *"Now steady on – stop rushing to conclusions like that. There is no evidence that it was murder, not an accident."*

She took a deep breath and went over the facts. It really was unlikely that Sam's father would have fallen asleep, but it was likely that someone wanted him dead.

Alice Hanson tidied up the files of old newspapers and returned them to the librarian.

"Thank you so much," she said. *"It was kind of you to help me find the*

ones I wanted," and still thinking hard, she headed back to her friend, Jack Riley's home.

Jack was an old bachelor who had always lived on his own except for his time in the Royal Marines before he progressed through, *'cloak and dagger'* military operations to the secretive work of MI5, the military intelligence service, and he had made some sandwiches for lunch.

"Well, what did you discover?" he asked Alice.

"I'm not sure," she answered, and went on to tell him that she was beginning to think that the crash which had killed Sam's father was not an accident.

Jack thought for a bit.

"The other car. That's the thing. Why didn't the driver tell the police what he might know? Even if it was only that he had overtaken Sam's father's car and hadn't seen it go off the road. What about the CCTV cameras? They should have his number. No – blast it – there aren't any along that stretch of the road."

The two of them munched on the sandwiches in grumpy silence. Then suddenly, Alice Hanson broke the silence.

"But Jack, if that other car did have anything to do with the crash, it must have been following Sam's father's car for some time – probably since they left London – and they passed a hell of a lot of cameras on their way."

"Alice, as usual, you're right. We had better get on to some of our old friends in the Metropolitan Police. They are not supposed to cough up information to just anybody, but I think we've done some of them enough favours in the past to ask for one back. I'll start on that this afternoon."

"Thanks," said Alice. *"And I think I'll have to go to Canine Partners. I want to find out a bit more about Sam and that dog."*

Jack looked at her very sharply. *"Alice – you are not coming quite clean with me are you? You are more interested in that dog than I've ever known you to be in any animal of any kind. What is it all about?"*

She smiled very sweetly at him and put on her most innocent little old lady look before saying, *"Now Jack. You've got quite enough to do without worrying about that dog. He "is just a bit odd, but you need not know any more than that for the time being. Bye, bye. I'll see you this evening."*

With that, she headed for the door, leaving Jack shaking his head muttering, *"She hasn't changed a bit in all the years I've known her!"*

Alice Hanson got into her car, thought for a moment, got out her mobile 'phone, looked down through the list of numbers and rang Canine Partners.

"Could I speak to Clive Baker's secretary?" she asked, and as soon as Jean answered the 'phone, she said in her most authoritative voice, *"Mr Baker please – it is Miss Hanson. He will remember me – I called him to say that Ben, the yellow Labrador, was looking for him."*

"He certainly will," thought Jean, as she asked Alice Hanson to hold on.

"Clive," she said as Clive Baker picked up the 'phone. *"Clive, it is that old lady, Miss Hanson, who told you that Ben was waiting to be collected from the police in Exeter. You remember she rang the other day. She wants to talk to you again."*

"Oh, no. I hope to God she isn't going to tell me there's another bloody dog looking for me. You had better put her through."

"Good afternoon," he added as Alice Hanson came on the line. *"You haven't got another dog asking to come here to find me have you?"*

"No – no – but I would like to come to meet you. Now let's see – it is about two o'clock – it will take me about two and a half hours to get to you. So I'll see you at about four thirty."

"Well, let me think," started Clive, but before he could think, Miss Hanson had thanked him and rung off leaving him looking at the 'phone as though it had just bitten him.

"Oh Hell – oh, bloody Hell," he was shouting as Jean looked around his office door, shook her head and said, *"Not another dog?"*

"Even worse," Clive snorted. *"She says she's coming here herself at half past four today."*

"If you don't want to see her, why did you agree to her coming?" asked Jean.

"I don't – and I didn't – but that won't stop her – she is some sort of one woman Panzer tank regiment – she just rolls over whatever is in her way."

Jean smiled to herself. She had often heard people call Clive something like that, and she found she was already looking forward to seeing some sort of tank battle when Miss Hanson arrived.

True to her word, Alice Hanson pulled into the car park at Canine Partners spot on 4.30 pm and made her way to Clive Baker's office. Jean, his secretary, asked her to take a seat, then knocked on Clive's door, looked in and said quietly,

"No luck – she didn't get lost – she's here."

Getting up from his desk, Clive mumbled, *"Then show her in."*

As she came in he nodded towards the chair by his desk and politely invited her to take a seat, asked if she would like a cup of tea and, as she thanked him, what he could do for her?

"Well," she started. *"I really wanted to enquire about Ben, but I'm ashamed to say, until I met him, I had never heard about Canine Partners. The more I learn about it, the more I admire what it does – and now I find that it is run by a former Royal Marine."*

Clive looked surprised. *"How did you know?"* he began.

Alice interrupted him – *"I recognised your tie. In fact, I'm staying with a very old friend of mine, Jack Riley, who was a Royal Marine too."*

Clive's surprise got the better of him and he broke into her words.

"Jack Riley? I was with him in the Commandos and the Special Boat Squadron and all sorts of things."

Alice repeated his words with some emphasis on the word, 'all'. *"All sorts of things – Hmm – I met Jack Riley when I was doing <u>all</u> sorts of things too. What a small world... But let's come back to why I came to see you. How much did you learn about Ben?"*

Clive looked very hard at her. *"How much do you know about him?"*

"That he came from Russia," she answered very quickly adding, *"And what did he tell you?"*

Without thinking, Clive replied, *"Just about everything. He said his master, Boris sent him here."* Then his voice died away as he realised that he was telling Alice Hanson something that was clearly unthinkable – that a dog had told him its unlikely life story.

Alice smiled reassuringly.

"No, Mr Baker – I know you are not mad. Nor am I. We both know that dog can communicate. It can't actually talk – but in some ways it can do even better. I'll come clean with you and tell you all that I know if you'll do the same."

"That's a bargain," Clive responded. *"But I've told no-one else about all this. Not even the boy – what about you?"*

"I've told no-one else," she reassured him. *"So I'll start at the beginning..."*

and she recounted all that she knew, and Clive did the same.

There was a pause. Then Alice Hanson spoke again.

"What about the boy? Wasn't it a bit of a risk to give the dog to him? What did you know about him? What does he know about the dog?"

Clive drew a deep breath. *"I'm still not sure what I should have done – but it was his old master, Boris, who had sent him here and told him he should become a care dog. Of course, I thought I would have loved to have had him when I was working with the security service – but Boris seemed quite clear he did not want Ben's gift just used by the police or security services – nor for him to finish up in a circus or TV show. He could have stayed here helping us to train dogs – but I don't think Ben himself would have wanted that. Then just at the time Ben arrived here, I had a call from the boss of the Spinal Injuries Unit at Stoke Mandeville Hospital, Mr Shah. He had looked after Sam after the car crash that killed his father and he asked me if I could find a dog for the boy. It was a terrible time for the boy. His mother had left his father and taken Sam and his sister to live with her new partner, George. He was pretty upset about that. Then the crash that crippled Sam killed his father and he really needed a friend who would never let him down. I did not really have to make a decision. It made itself."*

Alice nodded. *"I see. But did you tell the boy the truth about Ben? Does he know the secret of Ben's gift?"*

"I didn't tell him. I thought it best to let Ben decide when and how to do that. He's no fool that dog."

They sat in silence for a minute or so before Alice Hanson spoke very quietly.

"Clive," she said, *"If I may call you that. There is something more you should know. I've been doing a little research about Sam's father, his uncle, a drug addict, who died a few years ago, and the car crash. I'm not sure it was an accident. I think his father knew too much for his own safety about one of the big drug smuggling and selling gangs."*

"Why are you telling me all this?" asked Clive.

Alice got up and opened the door to leave, then paused before answering.

"Goodness me. Look at the time – I'll be late for dinner. Oh, why did I tell you all that? Well Clive, if you were a friend of my friend, Jack Riley, I sort

of guessed you would be interested. You must have worked with him in the Caribbean breaking up the drug cartels down there. I'll remember you to Jack. Goodbye."

And before Clive had time to say anything more, she was gone and he heard her car leaving the yard rather quickly for a little old lady.

When he looked up, his secretary, Jean, was standing by her desk with a puzzled look on her face.

"Clive, I really do despair of you since that lady and that dog came into your life. You didn't want to see her – she barged her way in – then you were nattering away as if you were old friends – and then she walks out before you had time to say goodbye."

"Oh bloody Hell," said Clive very quietly with his head in his hands. "I just don't think I'm quite in control of things. I think I'll go home."

Alice was well on her way back to Tring when she realised she had been driving faster than she had done for years. She felt younger too and realised how much she missed working in the security services. As the miles went by she was becoming more determined to discover the truth about that car crash. The next step was to talk to Sam and Ben, and the sooner the better.

By the time she got back to Tring, however, she was feeling that she had had a pretty full day and was looking forward to dinner.

Jack Riley greeted her with a cheerful, "I hope you had a good afternoon. Was it worth the drive?"

"Oh yes – I learned a lot about Canine Partners and about the boy – and I met one of your old friends from your Royal Marine Commando days – Clive Baker – he runs Canine Partners."

"What – Clive!" exploded Jack Riley. "Running a school for dogs – what a change from ambushing the drug traders when we were down in the Caribbean. Fancy that. But I've something to tell you. There was dirty work involved in that car smash."

"What did you find out then?" asked Alice.

Jack drew a deep breath.

"Quite a lot. You know that the boy and his father went to a cinema in the Haymarket in the West End of London. They had left the car parked in Waterloo Place, just north of St James' Park. The other car which had been *following them must have been parked there too and it followed them all the way up Park Lane, onto the A41 at Swiss Cottage, all the way until just after they crossed the North Circular Road at Brent Cross. Then another car that had been parked at Brent Cross picked them up and followed them all the way to Hunton Bridge. After that they were on that fast dual carriageway – well, it's like a motorway, but there are no cameras on it – until the crash up near Berkhamstead only a few miles from Sam's home."*

"*Suspicious,*" said Alice.

"*There is more to it than that,*" continued Jack. "*The cameras picked up the car on the way back into town too, not long after the crash.*"

"*Who owns the cars?*" asked Alice.

"*Both owned by the same company, International Grain Transport & Trading – quite a big business buying, selling, importing and exporting wheat, barley and all that. But here's the most interesting thing of all. The car that followed Sam's father's car to the scene of the crash was sold a couple of days later. I got all this from the Drive and Vehicle Licensing Centre at Swansea. They are very helpful to the police and, as you know, I've got friends there so I didn't have to wait weeks for the information or hunt for it on the internet. They told me that the car dealer who bought it is a bit dodgy, and within a few days he reported it damaged beyond repair and scrapped it after it had caught fire. That really is odd as it was a big BMW only about a year old – unless there was forensic evidence – like paint off Sam's father's car on it.*"

Alice had taken in every word of Jack's report, and thought carefully before she spoke.

"*Jack – it looks pretty clear doesn't it? It wasn't an accident. It was murder. That BMW pushed Sam's father's car off the road. And they got rid of it to get rid of the evidence. And whoever did it didn't care if they had killed Sam too.*"

Jack got up from his chair. "*Alice,*" he said. "*It's time we had something to eat. It's getting late and we had better think what we do next.*"

"*I have,*" retorted Alice. "*Even while you were talking. I must talk to the boy – very soon – in the next day or so if we can. It won't be hard to discover the murderer – we can be pretty sure of the motive – Sam's father knew too much. But getting the killer convicted and sent to jail will not be so easy. But you're right. It's dinner time.*"

CHAPTER TWELVE

PRIZEGIVING

S omewhat to his mother's surprise, Sam was up early and ready for his breakfast by 7.30 on Tuesday morning.

"Have you forgotten, there is no school this morning?" she asked. *"It's Prizegiving and you don't need to be there until 2 o'clock."*

"No, I'd not forgotten," Sam reassured her. *"But I thought I should take Ben down to the park and then bring him back for a good brush. He is coming with me to collect my prize so we had both best look smart."*

His mother just nodded, but she smiled to herself thinking that the dog did seem to be a good influence on her son.

Breakfast over, Sam and Ben headed for the park. Along the way, as they had agreed the previous night, if there were other people about, Ben either said nothing or whispered very softly, whilst Sam talked quite normally, as all good masters talk to their dogs.

Like most paraplegics (who have no use of their legs), Sam's shoulders and arms had become much stronger and Ben had a wonderful time chasing and catching his ball, until Sam called out –

"Time to go Ben – we must get cleaned up and dressed before lunch."

Neither of them had noticed the little old lady who had come into the park to watch them, and now hurried out, keeping well ahead of them. She got into her car and drove away before they had reached the gate. But as Sam propelled his chair along the path towards the gate, Ben suddenly stopped, sniffing first at the air and then the ground.

"Master, Master. Stop – there is something very odd. You remember I told you about the old lady who helped in the town called Exeter – she has been here. I can smell her. She was here only minutes ago."

"Are you sure?" questioned Sam.

"Yes Master – Labradors do not make mistakes about such things."

They looked around, but there were few people in sight – and no old ladies. She was gone, but her scent was there to be detected by a good dog's nose.

"That is very strange," said Sam. *"But we had better get home and I'll give you a good brush."*

By the time Sam had had lunch and they were ready to set off to the school he had quite forgotten about the old lady. Ben, however, was still trying to think why she should have been in the park in Tring. Dogs like things and people to fit into patterns and to them anything that doesn't fit might mean danger; so Ben was extra alert. His nose, ears and eyes were all searching for anything which might threaten Sam.

They all walked to school together, Sam, Sophie, their mother, George and, of course, Ben, looking very good in his best yellow Canine Partners jacket. When they got there the hall was already crowded, but a place was reserved for Sam and Ben in the front row of seats, just by the ramp for them to go up onto the stage.

Ben was a bit bored as he did not really understand a lot of the talk going on and although he was still puzzled about picking up the scent of the old lady from Exeter that morning in the park, he did what any sensible dog would do at a school prizegiving; he went to sleep. He missed all the speeches about how well the school had done and the news of old boys and girls who were making their way in their new careers.

He did not even stir as the Headmaster, "Scruffy" Brown, introduced the guest speaker, Sir John Munday, a very successful local businessman whose company, International Grain Transport & Trading, bought, sold, imported and exported thousands of tons of cereal crops – wheat, barley and rye. More important to the school, he had given thousands of pounds to equip new science labs and as he was a very keen swimmer, to rebuild the school's swimming pool.

Sam thought his talk was quite interesting, all about the importance of international trade, but he thought Sir John sounded just a bit arrogant and he heard George, who was sitting behind him, mutter something about money not being able to buy everything that matters.

Then it came to the prizegiving. The Headmaster read out the name of each prize winner and what the prize was for, and handed it to Sir John. He said a few words to the recipient, shook hands and handed over the prize. It took a little while with the form prizes coming first, then the examination certificates and the sports prizes, and then the special awards for things like services to the school and almost at the very end, Sam's award.

The Headmaster looked straight at Sam and read out aloud:

"For overcoming adversity, Sam Turner – who, after his terrible injury and the loss of his father – has returned to school and resumed his studies despite being wheelchair bound."

The mention of Sam's name woke Ben just in time to help Sam charge up the ramp and onto the stage. "Stuffy" Brown handed to Sir John Munday a copy of Sam's father's book, *'Crooks, Drugs and Dirty Business'*. As he took the book from the Headmaster, Sir John glanced at the title and went quite white. Sam and the Headmaster thought for a moment that he had been taken ill as he almost dropped the book, but he recovered, and shaking Sam's hand, gave it to him. But he did so without looking straight at the boy.

Sam managed to say, *"Thank you Sir,"* but Sir John only muttered something the boy could not quite catch. Then as Sam turned his wheelchair to go back down the ramp he realised that Ben was sitting staring hard at Sir John, his head held high, nostrils wide open and the hair on the back of his neck standing up like a brush.

"Ben – here Ben – here," snapped Sam, as he heard the softest of growls – but still definitely a growl, before Ben was back at the side of his wheelchair ready to help steady it on the ramp.

Back in their place, Sam felt Ben's nose pressed against him and it was all that he could do to stay silent. Why had Sir John looked at the book as though it might bite him? And why had Ben looked as though he might have bitten Sir John too?

It was a great effort, but Sam managed just to put his hand on Ben's nose and say,

"Good boy – be quiet – good boy."

In a few minutes more, the prizegiving was all over and everyone began to move around. Some people were talking to each other or to teachers and others were heading for the refreshments at the back of the hall.

Sam turned to his mother and George, suggesting that he should take Ben for a run in the park, adding,

"I'm sure Sophie will show you anything you want to see and find any of the teachers, but I think Ben needs a leak and we will see you back home."

And with that, the two of them were off – heading for the park.

Apart from normal words of command the pair were silent until reaching the favourite spot in the park where they could be sure that no-one else was close enough to overhear them.

Sam stopped his wheelchair. Ben put his front paws up on the boy's lap looking straight at him, as the boy said,

"Ben, Ben, old dog, what was that all about?"

The dog paused for a moment, then replied very quietly, but very firmly.

"Master – that man – the one who gave you the prize. He was scared by that book. I could smell fear on him. There was something on it that scared him so much he nearly dropped it."

Sam went to speak, but Ben cut him short. *"That is not all Master. That man was one of those who went into your father's flat. I have a very good memory for scent and I could smell that for sure – before he touched the book – and then the scent of fear blotted it all out. That is why I waited until that faded and I could make sure that it was his scent that was in your father's flat when we went there. Master, that man, Sir John. He is not a good man."*

Sam drew a very deep breath before he spoke.

"Ben, I don't know what to make of it all. Why was Sir John so scared or upset by my father's book? What was he doing breaking into the flat? Ben, you

*don't think he is a crook in the drug business? No Ben, surely he couldn't be?
Or could he? Could he be the leader of the gang that my father was after?"*

His voice tailed away and his head dropped as he tried to think – or
almost not to think – what it was all about.

Ben saw that his master was upset and worried. He pushed his muzzle
under Sam's chin to raise the boy's head, then looked squarely at him.

*"Master, I am a dog not a human and I do not understand these things.
I can only tell you what I know – sometimes things humans do not notice.
I'm sorry I can't do more."*

"Thank you old dog," said Sam. *"Thank you, but I do not know what to do
– or who to tell – and how can I tell them what you have told me without telling
them the secret of your gift?"*

"Master," he replied. *"My Master, Boris was a very, very clever man, and
he used to say, 'if you don't know what to do, don't do anything until you do –
otherwise you might do something very, very wrong'. You will work it out – or
something will happen that will show you what do. But it is getting late for tea.
I think we should go home."*

*"Oh, Ben – you are a good friend. I might even find you a bonio before
dinner. Thank you."*

Sam turned his wheelchair back towards the gate and along the road
to home.

That evening after dinner, Sam let Ben have a run on his own in the
garden and then after talking for a while to his mother, George and Sophie,
he decided to go to his room and read some of his father's book. He had
known well enough that his father knew a lot about the big time drug dealers,
but the book told the whole story of the drugs trade. Poor farmers in places
such as Afghanistan and Central America, grow most of the world's cocaine
and heroin poppies. The brutal local mafia style gangs are in it just for the
money in Central America and the Taleban extremists need drugs money to
finance their war against the British and Americans in Afghanistan. Then
there are smugglers – some in private yachts – some poor fools paid to
swallow the drugs in packets and travel by air to American and European
cities – sometimes dying when the packs leak and poison them, and finally,
the factories processing the raw drugs to sell on the streets, in clubs and even

schools, to trap users into drug addiction – and often, like Sam's uncle, a life of crime to get the money for more and more drugs ending their lives in a squalid early death in a squat.

Ben lay quietly beside Sam's chair, watching him closely as the boy turned the pages. He remembered how Boris sometimes seemed to be completely lost in a book, or when he was working, so much that Nikita could come into the room, even bringing food or a drink without his master looking up Now he realised Sam was doing the same.

All Ben could do was to wait, and with his nose just touching the wheelchair, so that Sam could not move without him knowing, he went to sleep.

It was quite two hours before Sam closed the book, looked down at Ben and whispered very quietly to him.

"Ben, Ben old dog. I really do not know what to think. That man, Sir John. He was frightened of this book – and he seemed frightened of me. I'm beginning to think that I need someone to help me find out the truth. That's what my father would have wanted."

"Master, you are right – but so was my master Boris. As I said in the park today, we must wait until you are sure who to trust. It is time for bed. Let me help you."

Sam nodded and as he turned his chair, Ben opened the bathroom door and stood aside.

CHAPTER THIRTEEN

SAM MEETS ALICE

Apart from watching Sam and Ben in the park, Alice had done nothing all Wednesday, except to discuss with Jack Riley how she should tell Sam what she had discovered about his father and the car crash. Finally, they had decided they would have to approach him in the park on the way home from school the next day.

So on Thursday afternoon, Jack Riley was grumbling to himself as he was jumping up and down, jogging round in small circles in the park as though he was a keep fit fanatic – which he certainly was not. All the time he was keeping watch for Sam to bring Ben into the park for his run on the way home from school.

Jack was just getting really out of breath when he spotted the boy and the dog coming down the path. Turning his back on them he spoke quietly into the microphone on his track suit collar.

"They have just come in Alice," he reported to Miss Hanson, who had been waiting in her car a little way down the road.

"And the wind is blowing from the gate so the dog will pick up your scent pretty quickly."

"*Good,*" said Alice as she got out of the car. "*I'm on my way,*" and moving quite quickly for an old lady, she reached the gates in no time at all.

Ben was even more alert than usual to any danger to his master. He was worried about Sir John and the book and still puzzled about picking up the scent of Alice Hanson the previous day.

He had been watching Jack Riley carefully, but he turned to glance up the path towards the gate just as Alice Hanson walked in. The hair on the back of his neck came up as he stiffened and stared as hard as he could. Dogs cannot see colour as we do and, except at night, when we can see very little in the dark and they see a lot, their vision is not as good as ours. But they do see anything moving, even a long way away, rather better than us and they recognise people they know by the way they move even half a mile away.

"*Master,*" he whispered softly. "*Master, I think that is the little old lady who helped me.*"

Then, as the breeze carried her scent down the path, he almost shouted, turned the shout into a bark and then speaking quietly lest the man jogging and jumping should hear, he added, "*Master – I'm sure it is – Master, I must find out why she is here. Come with me.*"

Almost without waiting to see if Sam was following, Ben was off rushing towards the old lady. She saw him coming, but hardly had time to even think that her plan was working before he was skidding to a stop in front of her, tail wagging.

"*Ben,*" she shouted, but completely forgetting his manners, the dog interrupted her.

"*Mistress – what are you doing here? How did you find me?*"

"*Oh Ben,*" Alice replied. "*I just had to find out what happened to you, and I wanted to meet your master Sam.*"

By this time Sam had caught up with Ben.

"*Hey dog,*" he interrupted. "*What was all that about? You are supposed to look after me – not leave me alone in the park.*" Then as he looked up to Alice Hanson he remembered his manners – even if Ben had forgotten his, and added.

"*Good afternoon – you must be the lady who found Ben in Exeter and took him to the police station.*"

"That's right – my name is Alice Hanson," and turning to Jack Riley who had quietly approached them, she added, *"And this is my friend, Jack Riley. He was almost as good at looking after me when I was working in all sorts of places, as Ben is at looking after you."*

In a moment or two everyone was introduced to each other, although Ben said nothing more, and then Alice turned to Sam.

"Sam – I think I have to talk to you. There is something you should know about your father. There is hardly anyone in the park cafe. Shall we go there for a cup of tea?"

Sam hesitated. Accepting such an invitation from the old lady – especially as she had helped Ben – was one thing, but with her friend, well, that was another matter.

"Does he have to come?" he asked very quietly. *"We have to keep Ben's secret."*

Somewhat to Sam's surprise, Alice began to smile. She turned to Jack Riley who was still standing a few paces away.

"Jack – the boy is no fool. He'll come for a cup of tea, but I think it best if you just keep looking after us from a safe distance." Jack nodded and Alice continued –

"Come on Sam and Ben – there is a lot to talk about."

There were not many people in the cafe and it was easy enough for Sam to find a table in a quiet corner. Alice Hanson had picked up a tray, bought some tea and biscuits and sat down opposite the boy. As Ben had realised when he had asked her for help in Exeter, although at first glance she looked just like any other old lady, Alice Hanson had an air of quiet authority.

As Sam thanked her for his tea and biscuits, she spoke in a very quiet voice.

"That's alright Sam. I think I must be quite honest with you. I am retired now, but I have a lot of friends who I worked with in the security services – some now retired like me and Jack; others still working. And you should know that Clive Baker, who you met at Canine Partners, was a Royal Marine commando, who worked for a time with Jack. We are all members of the same family. I am sure Ben has told you of his journey from Russia to join Canine Partners."

Ben gave a quiet growl of assent as Sam quietly said, *"Yes – he told me about you helping him too."*

Alice smiled. *"I really thought I was going daft when I realised I could hear Ben's voice in my head, but if he and his master Boris said he was to become a Canine Partner, I really had to help him. The trouble was that after I left him at the police station, I kept wondering what had happened to him. Eventually, I got in touch with Clive Baker and found out that Ben had gone to look after you.*

When I discovered that you lived here in Tring, I came to stay with my old friend Jack. I have not told him Ben's secret which is why I asked him to stay outside. Yesterday, with Jack's help, I found out about your father, about the car crash and a lot more."

She was watching Sam's face as she spoke and paused for a moment before she continued.

"Sam, you have been very brave..." But Sam interrupted her.

"Mr Shah told me that it would be very bad at first – but I could either beat it – or it would beat me. I remember him saying that my life would never be the same – but I could make a new life. And he promised he would find me a faithful friend to help me. He couldn't have known what a friend Ben would be."

Alice put her hand on Sam's and spoke very quietly.

"Sam, I don't think your father fell asleep – I don't think the crash was an accident. I think he was murdered and I think it was because he knew too much about the drug smugglers."

Sam cut in. *"He told us – that is my sister, Sophie and me – that he had almost all the evidence he needed and he was going to hand it over to the police very soon. I had begun to wonder if the smash was an accident too, but I can't remember anything about it."*

Alice continued. *"I think they found out about your father and I'm sure it was another car that forced him off the road, right where the bank down was very steep with big trees at the bottom. Jack found out for me the number of the car I think that did it, and who owned it..."*

Sam cut in, stopping her in mid-sentence.

"Be careful – oh – do be careful – if they found out they would kill you too..."
Alice shook her head.

"I doubt it," she smiled. *"Quite a lot of people have tried to do that, but*

no-one has managed it yet – and I don't think Jack would let that happen."

She looked down at Ben who had put his paw on her knee.

"*Master,*" Ben said very softly to Sam. "*Should you not tell her about the man, Sir John? He was frightened when he saw your father's book. He was frightened of you and he was one of the men who had been in your father's flat.*"

"*Mistress – he is a very bad man.*"

"*Who is Sir John?*" asked Alice, and Sam told her about the prizegiving day at school, how Ben had recognised Sir John's scent as that of one of the men who had broken into Sam's father's flat. Alice listened very quietly until right at the end, Sam said, "*It is hard to believe Sir John is a drug smuggler. He has given lots of money to our school and his Company is supposed to be very successful – it is called something like International Grain Trading.*"

Alice sat up very straight indeed. "*What?*" she said. "*Not International Grain Transport & Trading?*"

"*That's right,*" answered Sam. "*Is that important?*"

Alice took a deep breath. "*Sam – the car which I think pushed your father's car off the road was owned by International Grain Transport & Trading. There's no doubt about it. Ben is quite right. Sir John is a very bad man indeed. He is up to his neck in all this.*"

Then she took a very deep breath.

"*Sam, Ben – you must both trust me. I need to think this out and I need to do that before Sir John gets suspicious. Look, it is getting late and your mother will be worried about where you have got to. I'm just thinking very quickly, but I'm beginning to see what to do. Don't say anything at home about all this. With a bit of luck, I'll persuade Clive Baker to say that I work for Canine Partners and that I'll be coming to see how you and Ben are getting on. If I do, don't let on that you already know me. Anyway, I'll find you on your way to or from school if needs be. Now, don't worry. You two have done a good job. Now it is up to me to plan how to trap Sir John and smash his drug gang.*"

"*Thank you – thank you. May I call you Alice?*" asked Sam very politely.

"*Of course,*" she said. "*But only when we and Ben of course, are on our own. Sam – you are a very tough and grown up young man. It will be great to help you put these people where they deserve to be. Come on – let's get home.*" In a moment she was up and out of the cafe.

Ben and Sam looked at each other.

"*Wow!*" they both said at once. "*What a lady.*"

By the time they were out of the cafe, Alice and Jack were gone.

"*Time for dinner Ben,*" said Sam, and they hurried home, thinking hard about what might happen next.

Once they were home, Sam told his mother that he had a lot of homework to get done before dinner time and took a cup of tea into his room. Ben closed the door behind them and they looked at each other for a moment or two before Ben said very quietly, "*Master – what do you think Alice and her friends are going to do?*"

Sam thought for a few moments and sighed.

"*I don't think I know Ben. But I do know she is a very unusual old lady. Did you notice that Jack did whatever she said – and I think he is a pretty tough chap – and so is Clive Baker.*"

"*Yes Master – she is like my old master Boris. She is a pack leader. But what did she mean when she said that she, Clive and Jack are all in the same family?*"

Again, Sam took time to think before he replied.

"*I think Ben that they have all worked together in the secret service and they trust each other. And you are right. They are her pack – and she is the leader. She said she would 'think it all out'. I don't know what that means, but I think she wants to trap that man, Sir John.*"

Ben thought about that for a while and said, "*I think she will. She is very tough. But she will need you to help and we must wait for her,*" and he curled up under Sam's work table waiting for dinner time.

CHAPTER FOURTEEN

THE 1812 OVERTURE DISC

That evening as Jack and Alice finished dinner, Alice put her hands flat on the table and said,

"Well, Jack. We've got a really interesting problem here. What do you think?"

"I suppose the first thought that came to my mind was why not hand over the whole thing to the police...?" said Jack.

"And why not?" interrupted Alice. *"We don't have to be involved do we?"*

"No – but what evidence do we have?" Jack continued. *"Let's think what we do know. Sir John did behave oddly at the prizegiving. He is the boss of International Grain Transport & Trading. A car belonging to his firm followed Sam's father's car from London out to Brent Cross, and another followed it to somewhere past Watford. And we know that the second car was sold just after that to a dodgy dealer who said it caught fire and was a write-off. We can't prove the smash wasn't an accident. We can't prove Sir John had anything to do with it – or with drug smuggling."*

"That's a very good summary," said Alice. *"But either with the police or without them, I think we will have to set a trap for Sir John and let him drop himself right in it. There is no real rush. Sir John is not fool enough to do*

anything to the boy. He thinks he has got away with it. In the morning I'll go home and perhaps I'll call on poor Clive Baker again."

"And why would you do that Alice?" asked Jack. *"Just what is it about that dog that you need to discuss with Clive Baker?"*

Alice smiled, yawned and said, *"I think it's time for my bed. Goodnight Jack – thank you for dinner,"* as she got up and headed for the stairs.

At Canine Partners next day, Clive Baker was quietly looking through his lists of dogs in training and disabled people waiting for help dogs, thinking that things were going rather well when Jean, his secretary, looked round the door.

"Clive – I'm afraid it's her again – Miss Hanson – she wants to know if she could take you to lunch today on her way home from your friend, Jack Riley. She says she wants to tell you all the news."

"Oh my God – not that."

Jean cut him short. *"She says she knows you would enjoy that as she has a lot to tell you about Jack, Sam and Ben."*

Clive's every instinct told him to say 'No', yet somehow he found himself saying, *"Oh – oh – er – yes – about 1 o'clock at the pub – tell her where it is and I'll see her there – and book a table."*

Jean shook her head in disbelief, muttered, *"alright then,"* and left Clive still swearing that he never wanted to ever hear of a stray dog looking for him again. Not ever.

When Clive arrived at the pub, Alice was already there, tucked away in a quiet corner. She smiled as he sat down and thanked him for sparing her his time. Then almost before he had the chance to ask how he could help her, Alice said –

"I've got a favour to ask of you. Would you take me on as a Canine Partners helper? I need to be able to talk to Sam and Ben and take them out without giving away what we are up to."

Inevitably, Clive asked what she was up to, without really expecting an answer. Much to his surprise, Alice smiled and said –

"Let's order our lunch and I'll tell you the whole story – but just as it was when you worked with Jack; tell no-one unless they really need to know. If we are not careful, someone might get killed."

They ordered their lunch in something of a hurry and once the waiter was out of earshot, Alice began to tell him all she had learned from Sam and Ben, the newspaper reports about Sam's father and from Jack about the cars that had followed them on the night of the crash.

"Clive," she said. "They mustn't get away with it, but I think it will take a pretty smart bit of skullduggery to put that lot behind bars. The police will never do it on their own. If they ever got near him, Sir John would be off to Columbia or somewhere, like a shot. We have to plan a sting to get him to incriminate himself, but the police just can't do that. It is up to us."

It was almost an hour later before they got up from the table. Alice thanked Clive, saying it had been useful to pick his brains. Then as they parted she added –

"Don't forget to let Sam's mother know that you'll be sending me to make sure Ben and Sam are getting along alright. And don't hesitate to talk to Jack – but remember – I have not told him yet about Ben's secret. Goodbye."

"How was the lunch?" Jean asked Clive as he arrived back at his office. To her surprise, he smiled. "Oh lunch – yes – lunch – oh, very interesting – very interesting. Oh Jean, Miss Hanson is going to sort of join Canine Partners as one of our voluntary visitors – but she will only visit Sam and Ben. She'll let us know when, and we'll arrange it with Sam's mother. She gave me her address and all that, so may I leave it to you to fix it all up. Now, I'd better go to see how the training is going. I'll be back for tea."

Clive was out of the office before his secretary Jean could say anything and she was left looking at his back as he hurried away.

"Between them," she muttered, "that dog and that woman seem to have driven him out of his mind."

Alice Hanson was more than pleased to get back to Tring after a long slow journey on the M25. The traffic had been too heavy for her to think much about making plans to deal with Sir John and the drug racket, and she was glad to sit down with Jack Riley to tell him about her lunch with Clive Baker.

"That's fine," said Jack, as she finished. "So Clive knows as much about the car crash, Sir John and his company, International Grain Transport & Trading, and the drugs racket as we do. The question is, what do we do next?"

Alice took her time before she replied. "We know that at the school *prizegiving, once Sir John realised who Sam was, he nearly collapsed with fright. He is a coward and he is scared he might be caught for the murder of Sam's father."*

Jack nodded. *"But just how do we arrange that?"*

Again, Alice hesitated before she replied –

"What about the car? He knew there was enough evidence there to convict him. That's why he got that crooked car dealer to burn it. It must have been covered with his finger prints and DNA and paint from Sam's father's car. If he thought that the crooked dealer had sold it instead of burning it, then..."

Alice's voice faded away as Jack interrupted her.

"That's all very well – but if he thought that – he would be after the dealer like a shot."

Alice was silent for a moment.

"You're right Jack. But suppose the car dealer had done a runner and disappeared ...?"

Again, Jack stopped her.

"Come on Alice. Why would he do that?"

She looked at him and smiled.

"Come on Jack – we could persuade him – help him to disappear. Especially if he thought Sir John was after him."

"Alice," said Jack. *"Hold on. This isn't some third world dump in Africa. You can't just make people disappear and get away with it here. Anyway, we are retired now."*

"All the better," she replied. *"We don't have to account to anyone – so long as we aren't caught. But let's leave that for a moment. We have to convince Sir John that we have got the car and blackmail him. We could offer to sell it to him for a couple of hundred thousand pounds or so. If we got him to somewhere ... we can think about that later... and taped him – or even better, videoed him – Jack, you're looking doubtful."*

Jack nodded. *"That's because I am doubtful. I think the idea is okay, but there's a lot of work to fit it together – and who arrests him before he does a runner? We'll have to get the police on side ready to burst in, before he escapes or starts something silly. He might well turn up armed."*

"Let's have something to eat and tomorrow we can try to put some detailed

plans on paper. That's when we will see if it will work. And we can try calling some of our old friends from the drugs squad – they ought to be able to help."

Alice knew Jack well enough to know that he would not be pushed any further. The best thing was to agree to leave it until the morning.

Back at Sam's home, his mother was calling him to come and sit down for his dinner – and just as well thought Ben, who was getting hungry (as Labradors do) after his long day looking after his master. Although, at first when he had sat down at his desk, Sam could not stop thinking about Alice and Jack and Clive, after a minute or two, he realised that his mind was just going round in circles and he would have to get stuck into his homework. Within another few minutes, he began to find that the maths homework was really quite interesting. Once that was done, the history essay was pretty straight forward and he began looking through the text book, ready for the next week.

A gentle grumbling noise from Ben reminded Sam it was time for the dog's dinner. As usual, it was turkey and rice kibble, but as a treat Sam had saved some meat gravy, which Ben loved. Dinner for humans was pasta with meat sauce which Sam enjoyed, but as he put down his fork he realised that George had been looking very hard at him. He looked down at his plate to avoid making eye contact.

"Sam," said George. *"You are very quiet these days. Is there anything wrong? I asked your form mistress, Miss Scott, and she said you were doing fine – and she said Ben is doing well too. In fact she said that although Ben goes to sleep during maths and science he seems as interested as anyone in English and Geography."*

Ben kept his head down. He had not realised just how closely the teachers, especially Miss Scott, had been watching him. And he knew that what George had said was true. He could not make sense of maths, but he understood quite a lot of some other lessons and once or twice he had almost forgotten himself and answered a teacher's question.

Sam began to smile to himself and told George that there was nothing wrong – but added –

"But I do find it hard work catching up all that I missed while I was in hospital, but it is getting easier. And I couldn't manage at all without Ben. It is

very hard work being stuck in a wheelchair and I do get tired, so if you don't mind, I'll go back to my room, get ready for bed and listen to some of my father's tapes and CDs that I brought home from his flat. He had a terrific collection of music. Good night."

As the door closed, Sam's mother looked at George, but it was his sister Sophie, who spoke first.

"Sam has changed – but I think anyone would have after a terrible crash like that and then being in hospital for so long too. And it is hard work for him trying to stay up with his friends, but then sometimes he doesn't seem to care much about other people. I see him and Ben looking at each other as though they were sharing secrets just between themselves. That dog is very, very clever and Sam hardly seems to need other people."

"Well Sophie," said her mother. *"If Sam is doing well at school, there can't be too much worrying him. I think you're right. You know, I said the other night to George that he hardly needs anyone, apart from Ben. In fact, I think if that dog could cook and iron his shirts he wouldn't need us at all."*

Sophie nodded. *"And we both miss Dad – but Sam won't talk about that."*

As it happened, Sophie was not quite right, because Sam had been talking about his father, but only to Alice Hanson and of course, Ben. Indeed, at that very moment he was telling Ben that he had found one of his father's favourite CDs.

"It is the 1812 Overture by Tchaikovsky, Ben," he told the dog. *"It is really exciting music – here we go."*

Tchaikovsky's music crashed out from the great orchestra and Sam settled himself to listen when suddenly the music stopped. There was a pause and then it was Sam's father's voice.

"22 January 2009. I now have all the details of how the drugs business is covered up in the legitimate business of International Grain Transport & Trading. It is like a shadow of that business. The big players are Sir John Munday, Chairman and Chief Executive. The Deputy Chief Executive is Robert Finch. Below them there are two separate businesses. The people in the legitimate business of buying and selling wheat, barley, oats and rice, all work at the company headquarters in Milton Keynes. They know nothing about the drugs business. That is hidden at a warehouse in London docklands, but most

of the managers of that never meet each other. The senior buyer is in Spain..."

And so it went on – a long list of names, addresses and telephone numbers. It was almost boring, yet Sam realised that it was because of what his father knew, that he had been murdered. He switched off the CD player.

"Ben," he said. *"Ben, do you understand? They must have killed my father because they suspected that he knew too much about them. The CD shows he knew almost everything about them. They must have taken his notes and papers when they broke into the flat, but they didn't know he had concealed it all on this CD."*

A great crease came across Ben's head, from between his ears almost down to his nose, as he struggled to work out what it all meant.

"No Master. I don't understand all this, but I think it is very important. That man killed your father because he knew all these things and because he had that CD thing. Now you know these things and you have the CD. Master, if that man, Sir John, knew that, he might kill you. And if that was what he was looking for when he went to your father's flat, then he might come here if he thought it was here. I think you should hide that thing. Put it under the cushion in my basket. I will guard it. Then you must tell Alice. I think she will know what to do."

Sam rubbed the dog's ears. *"You're right Ben. You are a very wise dog. This is for Alice to think about. I hope she gets in touch very soon."*

CHAPTER FIFTEEN

ALICE BEGINS TO PLAN

Friday passed quickly at school. It was a day of lessons which Sam quite enjoyed –especially history and an afternoon of science experiments in the laboratories.

Despite all their worries, both Sam and Ben slept well that night, until Ben's internal alarm woke him on Saturday morning about five minutes before Sam's alarm rang. He shook himself quietly, opened the bedroom door, and went into the kitchen to ask Sam's mother to unlock the garden door for him. Within moments he was back from a quick visit to his gravel patch at the end of the garden and waiting beside Sam's bed as the alarm rang. Sam had no chance to just switch it off and snuggle down back to sleep. Ben's nose was under the duvet, pulling it back despite Sam's muttered protests.

Ben enjoyed the 'getting up' routine, helping his master from bed to wheelchair, then chair to bathroom and shower, finding his clothes, helping him dress (and putting on trousers is not easy when you are paralysed from your waist down), then getting Sam into his wheelchair ready for breakfast.

Although he was unable to join in team games like football, Sam did not want to be just left out and forgotten from school sports. Tring School were playing at home that morning, so he was on his way there soon after breakfast to see his friends and cheer his team on.

Neither boy nor dog said anything on the way to school about Sam's discovery of his father's CD about Sir John Munday's drugs business, nor once the game had begun did Sam think much about it either. Ben, however, was still trying hard to understand what it all meant and how to find Alice, when they arrived at the school sports ground. He muscled a way through to a good place for Sam to watch the match, but as he could not join in, Ben was soon bored and his mind turned back to what Alice had said.

He had some idea of what drugs did to humans. His master Boris had told him that although drugs made humans stupid or even quite mad, they would steal or even kill each other to get them. Ben could not understand why humans could be both so much more clever and so much more stupid than dogs.

By their very nature, dogs are loyal to their masters just as in the wild they are loyal to the leader of their pack and dog packs have laws – just as we humans do. Ben realised that Sir John had broken the laws of the human pack and that not just Sam, but Alice and her friend were determined he would be punished for that.

It was all very complicated and he was wondering how that would happen and what he and Ben would have to do when he fell asleep. Suddenly he realised that Sam was talking to him.

"Come on old dog," Sam was saying. *"The game is over. Let's get home for lunch or would you like a run in the park on the way?"*

What a silly question, thought Ben. What sort of dog would say no to a run in the park?

Not far away, at Jack Riley's house, Alice had been doing some thinking too. That morning, over a late breakfast, she had turned to Jack Riley with a half smile.

"Well then Jack – what master plot have you hatched to catch Sir John?"

Jack thought for a while before he replied –

"I haven't. You might be right and we may have to make him believe that we have the car and offer to sell it to him. We might be able to say enough to prove he was in the car, even if not driving it, when it pushed Sam's father's car

off the road..."

Alice cut him short.

"That's all very well. That's what I said yesterday. But how do we stop Sir John going after the dodgy car dealer who he told to destroy it? Come on Jack, you said yesterday that wouldn't work – and it wouldn't."

Jack sighed. *"Well it might. He might not believe the car dealer. Anyway, what is your plan?"*

It was Alice's turn to look uncomfortable.

"Surely we are not just going to the police? Even if they believed us and they arrested Sir John for the drugs racket – would they have enough evidence to get him for the murder of Sam's father? We know that his company, International Grain Transport & Trading, is the cover for a huge drugs business – and we know that because Sam's father had gathered all the evidence to put Sir John Munday and his friends behind bars. Munday either killed him or paid someone else to do it for him."

"But we haven't got the evidence Sam's father had. We don't know how much he has written down and we don't know if Sir John and his boys found it when they burgled the flat. In short, we don't know enough for the police to go for him and we don't know enough to set a good trap."

Both Jack and Alice were silent for a while. Then Alice got up.

"Jack," she said. *"If Sam's father had the evidence, where is it now? Sir John is very scared of something to do with Sam's father. We know that from what Sam told us about the prizegiving. So what is he going to do next? He knows he almost gave himself away at the prizegiving. If he thought that Sam knew too much – well, I don't like to think what he might do in a panic."*

"I ought to see the boy – but it's Saturday, so I may not find him as easily as if he was at school and I don't know if Clive at Canine Partners has told Sam's mother that I am one of his staff, checking up that the boy and the dog are okay. I think I'll walk down to the park in case Sam goes there with Ben. I'll see you later."

And with that she got up, put on her coat and was gone, leaving Jack still at the table. He waited until she was well on her way before following her to the park.

Alice had already been round the park and she was wondering whether to go back to Jack's home or for a cup of coffee in the park cafe, when Sam and Ben turned into the park gateway.

Ben sniffed at the ground, then lifted his head to sniff at the air.

"Master," he said very quietly. *"I think Alice has been here today."*

Then as Sam had begun to ask, *"Is she still...?"* Ben let out a proper bark – loud enough for Alice to turn round, see them and wave.

Within moments they were all together outside the cafe, then with greetings exchanged, Alice suggested coffee for Sam and herself and perhaps a digestive biscuit for Ben. They had hardly settled at a table in a quiet corner before Alice began.

"Sam, Jack and I don't think we have enough evidence to go to the police, but we think we could trap Sir John. We would probably have to pretend that we had the car which pushed you and your father off the road. He paid someone to burn it because it would incriminate him. There would be his DNA in it and paint from your father's car on it, but it won't be easy and we many need you to scare him again too – and that could be dangerous..."

Sam who was listening intently to Alice, looked down as Ben put a paw on his knee.

"Master," Ben interrupted. *"You should tell Alice about the music and your father's voice. I think that is important."*

Alice stopped in mid-sentence, looking first at Ben, then at Sam.

"What's that? Your father's voice Sam?"

Sam took a deep breath.

"Ben's right. It is important and I was going to tell you. Last night I put on one of my father's discs – it was a favourite of his – the 1812 Overture – but after a minute or two the music stopped and it was my father..."

Sam stumbled over his words. Ben laid his muzzle on the boy's lap and Alice just said very quietly, *"It's alright Sam – take your time."*

Sam took another deep breath and looking down at Ben, he continued.

"It was dated January of this year – and he described how Sir John's drugs business was hidden inside International Grain. He listed all the names and telephone numbers of the people running the drugs racket, what they did... I didn't listen all through. It was just like a telephone directory..."

By then Alice was sitting up very straight indeed. *"Sam, Sam..."* she stopped him going on. *"Sam – did you try any more of his music discs?"*

"No," said Sam. *"Should I have done?"*

Alice shook her head. *"No, I don't think it will matter – it sounds to me as though we have everything we need. What did you do with the disc?"*

Ben looked up. *"It's in my bed, Mistress. I told Sam I would look after it. I think it must be what that man, Sir John was looking for when he went into Sam's father's flat. If he knew Sam had it, he would come to steal it. Alice, he is a very bad man."*

"And you," she said, *"are a very good dog – and a very smart one too. You are right. Sir John killed Sam's father because he knew too much about the drugs business and I'm quite sure he would kill anyone – or (and she smiled at Ben) any dog who got in his way. We had best not lose too much time. If Sir John found out – or guessed – what is on that disc, we might be in trouble."*

"Sam, you had better let me have it. He would never suspect that. I think I should come to see you next week at your home. I will get Clive Baker to 'phone your mother to say that I am one of Canine Partners' welfare visitors coming to make sure Ben is alright."

Sam nodded agreement, but wriggled a bit in discomfort at giving up something which had brought back so many memories of his father. *"But Alice – how will all this end? Shouldn't we let the police know everything we know about Sir John and leave it to them?"*

Alice drew a deep breath.

"Sam, the trouble is that your father is not here to give evidence and the last thing we want is for Sir John to be sent to trial and get off. We still need to trap him good and proper."

Ben was looking back and forth at Sam and Alice, with that great furrow running over his head, between his eyes and almost onto his snout.

"Mistress Alice," he said. *"I don't understand these things, but my old master Boris used to say that to trap rats you have to let them smell some good bait. That disc thing is what the man, Sir John was looking for at Sam's father's flat. Could that be the bait and the trap be the flat?"*

Alice almost dropped her tea.

"Ben – you are the most extraordinary dog. That is just what I was beginning to think. And I know just the man to lay the bait. My friend, Jack Riley. But we

will need the police to be there – and we need to frighten Sir John so that he gives the game away. Mind you, getting him into the flat looking for the disc won't be easy. Jack and I need to work that out. And between us – especially as Jack has worked with the drugs squad in the past – we should get the police there."

With every moment, Alice seemed to be getting less of a gentle old lady and more like the top secret agent she had been before she retired.

Sam still looked a bit doubtful, but Ben's tail was wagging even though he was sitting down.

No one else in the cafe would have given the old lady, the boy and the dog much of a second glance. They looked such an ordinary trio. Certainly no one would have guessed that the three of them were planning to bring the killer of the boy's father to justice and to smash one of the biggest drug rackets in Britain, and in a way, that was the biggest advantage they had.

Sam's mind was in something of a whirl. It was only a year or two earlier that he had been an ordinary schoolboy, living in an ordinary house in an ordinary family. Then it had all begun to fall apart as his mother and father quarrelled more and more often. Then George began to appear and suddenly, Sam's mother took him and Sophie to live with George. And then – and then – the terrible disaster, the car crash that had killed his father and left him paralysed, unable to walk and wheelchair bound.

Now it had all begun to change again. And it had all happened so quickly once he had met Ben. That was less than three weeks ago. And it was only last Tuesday that he had learned Ben's secret and only three days ago that he had met Alice.

Sometimes he dreamed that life was still the way it was before his parents parted, but it was always the same when he woke and his legs wouldn't move. Now he was wide awake – but he could hardly believe that this old lady, Alice, was planning to put the man she said had killed his father, in prison.

Yet somehow it all was horribly true – and it was just as his father had told him. It was all about drugs and money and the power they had to destroy lives. Not just his uncle's life, but his father's too. And now Alice was warning him it could even cost him his life.

He realised that Alice and Ben were looking hard at him.

"Are you alright Sam?" Alice was asking. He pulled himself together.

"*Yes, yes, I'm alright. It's just that everything is happening so quickly. I must think about all this.*"

Ben spoke very softly. "*Sam, it's time we went home. Alice will come there soon to see us. Until then you must just go on as usual. I will guard the disc thing. Alice and Jack will work out a plan...*"

"*That's right Ben.*" Sam silenced him by laying a finger on his nose. "*Alice, will you excuse us? I'm sure Ben is right. The place to get Sir John is my father's flat. It still has most of his things there because my mother doesn't want to use it, and she doesn't want to sell it. I know where the keys are so I could take them without telling her and let you have them.*"

"*That's enough Sam. You are learning bad habits,*" the old lady said. "*Ben is right. It's time you went home.*"

Over that weekend Sam, Alice Hanson and Jack Riley were all thinking how they could trap Sir John Munday. Sir John was thinking hard too. He had the feeling that he was not in control of things. Drug trading was one thing – alright, people did die from the drugs – they stole, robbed and even killed for the money to buy drugs, but that was their business he told himself. No one made them take drugs, but murder he had to admit was another.

He should have got someone else to kill Sam's father, but he had been so angry (and frightened) when he realised the man he knew as Barry – one of his best dealers – was really Charles Turner, the TV crime investigator – that he determined to do the job himself and quickly too.

The trouble was that at least three or four people knew that he was driving the car that pushed Sam's father's car off the road, killing him and crippling Sam. Suppose one of them began to blackmail him – or come to that, what if that boy found the evidence his father had collected while working in Sir John's business?

Sir John would have been much more worried had he known about the 1812 Overture disc on which Sam's father had concealed the details of the drugs racket. Or if he had known about Sam, Ben and their friends.

The more Sam had thought about it, the more he thought that Ben was right. Somehow that disc would become the bait in the trap, and the trap itself would be in his father's flat. What he could not work out was how to get Sir John to take that bait – or what would happen then.

A couple of miles away at Jack Riley's house, he and Alice Hanson were still thinking not only how to get Sir John to take the bait – but how the trap would be sprung.

Eventually Alice said, *"Jack – we are going round in circles. I don't think we can get any further until I've seen Sam and got hold of that 1812 Overture disc and you've talked to your friends in the police. Then we must go to look at Sam's father's flat. And we need to talk to the boy and the dog."*

Jack nodded – then said quietly, *"Talk to the boy and the dog,"* and with an emphasis on both the word 'talk' and the word 'dog'. *"Alice, am I imagining it or is there something odd about that dog?"*

Alice shifted uneasily. *"I feel a bit awkward about this because neither of them wanted you to know – but I suppose even saying that gives the game away a bit. Yes, there is something odd about Ben. He is a lot smarter than any other dog I've ever met – and yes, he does understand just about every word you say – and yes, he can communicate – in fact you can have a conversation with him."*

"I see," said Jack. *"I see – I'll ask no more – but of all the outlandish things I've ever met, a talking dog is just about the most unlikely – but I'll believe you Alice. So when do we all get together?"*

"I'll talk to Clive at Canine Partners tomorrow. He'll tell Sam's mother that I work for Canine Partners and that I will call to make sure Sam and Ben are getting on alright. I'll get the disc and we can listen to that. We need the keys to the flat and all four of us will have to go there together. It's one thing to get Sir John there – it's another thing to decide what to do next. He might be quite dangerous. But for now there is nothing to do but to get some lunch."

It did not take Alice long on Monday morning to get Clive – or to be more accurate Clive's secretary, Jane, to make an appointment for Alice to meet Sam and Ben as they left school the next day and walk home together for Alice's visit.

Ever since they had discovered the truth about Sir John, Ben had been extra careful, always looking out for any danger to his master. However, being a dog, not a human, he put any thoughts about how they would trap Sir John to the back of his mind. Sam found that much harder, so he was pleased when his mother told him on Monday evening that *"a lady called Miss Hanson is coming from Canine Partners to make sure that you and Ben are getting along alright.*" His mother said that Miss Hanson would meet him at school next afternoon and come home for tea.

By now, between them, Sam and Ben had learned to work together so well that Sam could keep up with the other pupils in his class in almost everything. Boys of fourteen are not usually very tidy or well organised, but Sam had no choice. Because everything he needed to do was more difficult and took longer than when he could walk he had to be well organised and so did Ben. As a result, Sam was rapidly catching up on the school work he had missed whilst he had been in hospital – and Ben had been picking up quite a lot during English, geography and history lessons too. Maths, of course, was quite beyond him and hard as he tried he could make absolutely nothing from either Sam's books or anything that teachers wrote on the blackboards.

He had also learned to conceal just how much he did understand, although it was not easy to fool Sam's form mistress, Miss Scott. He had learned not to even look as though he knew the answer when she asked the class a question. Nor even when she added, as she often did, *"Come on now. Surely you know the answer – even Ben does, don't you Ben?"*

On that Tuesday Ben had tried very hard indeed to keep his head down, but he was quite excited at the thought of seeing Alice Hanson again. So too was Sam, and at the end of the last period of the school day they scurried out of the classroom with Ben carving a way for Sam's wheelchair through the crowds of other pupils in the corridor, out down the ramp and across the playground to the school gates.

Sure enough, there was Alice Hanson. She had parked her car not far from Sam's home and walked back to the school to meet them. Ben bounded up to her with a series of joyful whooping barks with Sam following him shouting, *"Alice – I'm so pleased to see you."*

The greetings over, the three of them started the walk home. *"My mother said she would have tea ready for us, so there is no need to go to the park to talk,"* Sam told Alice. *"And what about me?"* asked Ben. *"I could do with a quick visit there."*

Sometimes he felt, when humans got together, they forgot the needs of the dogs, but as they came to the park gates Sam and Alice turned in and sent him racing across the grass into the woods, sniffing at all the scents and leaving his own for other dogs to read before the three of them resumed their walk to Sam's home.

Sam was pleased that his mother had made some fresh cakes for tea and once the introductions were over and they had sat down, Alice explained that she had to make an assessment of how well Ben was helping Sam.

"I cannot think how we could do without him," said Sam's mother. *"It is not just that he helps Sam get up, wash, dress and get to school, he makes sure Sam is always on time. He tidies the place up – and I think he is a very good bodyguard. I never worry about Sam if Ben is with him."*

Alice made a show of noting all this down between taking mouthfuls of cake – which was rather good. Indeed, Ben was watching every mouthful taken by everyone, hoping that some might fall on the floor.

"Could Sam show me his room and where Ben sleeps?" asked Alice.

"Of course," said his mother. *"And you'll see that they keep each other very tidy too. Go along Sam. Show Miss Hanson the way."*

Once they were in his room, Sam looked at the door saying quietly, *"Ben – the door – close it."* And in a moment Ben had pushed the door hard enough to click it firmly shut. The three of them looked at each other for a moment in silence.

Alice spoke first.

"Sam, Ben, I need the 1812 disc..."

"Yes Alice." Sam interrupted her. *"Ben says that has to be the bait in the trap for Sir John and he has been guarding it in his bed."*

Alice laughed. *"Ben, I'm sure you are right, but I need to hear just what Sam's father had found out about Sir John and the drugs business."*

Ben rummaged around in his bed, with his nose under the blanket and then with a little *"woof"* of satisfaction, found the disc, pulled it out and gave it to Alice.

"Do take care of it – and take care of yourself. I just know that Sir John is a very bad man."

Alice just smiled and gave Ben a rub behind his ears – something that all Labradors enjoy – as she turned back to Sam.

"Look Sam, we can't talk for long here, but we have to plan the sting to catch Sir John. I think it has to be at your father's flat. I'll have to think up a story for

your mother about why I have to take you to London – or perhaps I could tell her we were going to Canine Partners for something. My friend Jack, whom you met in the park, will be talking to his friends in the police because we will need their help, so there is a lot to do."

Sam had listened very carefully.

"Alright Alice, but when will we go to the flat and when will we set the trap for Sir John?" he asked.

She looked very thoughtful and spoke quite slowly.

"As soon as possible. We should visit the flat this weekend. How about Saturday? Now I'm sure that Jack could break into the flat, but that might waste a bit of time. And it is an extra risk. You never know, he might be mistaken for a burglar. Could you borrow the keys without your mother finding out?"

Sam nodded. *"I think so."*

Alice got to her feet. *"Right. Leave the rest to Jack, Clive and me. We will think of something when Jack reports back to me what he has arranged with his friends in the police. Now let's get back to the kitchen or your mother will wonder what we are up to."*

Sam looked at Ben, then without saying anything, at the door. Ben took the rope on the handle in his mouth, gave it a smart tug to unlatch the door and stood aside as, first Alice, then Sam, went out back to the kitchen.

Before Sam's mother could say anything Alice, with a big smile, said how pleased she was to see how happy Ben and Sam were and then, looking at them both added,

"I would like to take both of them back to Canine Partners quite soon to help sort out two or three other dogs and their masters who are not doing so well as Sam and Ben. Would you mind if I came to pick them up perhaps for just a day this weekend and another soon after?"

As it happened, Sam's mother and George had been wondering how to tell Sam that they wanted to take Sophie to start a training course on Saturday so they could all learn to sail small boats and then teach Sam too.

In no time at all she had agreed that Alice would pick up Sam and Ben the next Saturday morning.

Not for the first time Sam looked at Alice and thought she might look like an innocent little old lady, but she could think so fast and spin such a story even whilst she made it up as she went along. George had been so right to tell him not to judge people just on their appearance.

Later that night, after Sam and Ben had gone to bed, Sam's mother told George about Alice's visit and Sam's visit to Canine Partners.

"That solves a problem quite nicely," George observed. *"Now we need not tell him about our day out. But I think it is time we gave him a mobile 'phone. Most kids of his age have got them – and he needs one more than most – so I'll get one for him tomorrow."*

"Good idea," replied Sam's mother. *"And it will be a good thing for him to have something that dog can't do. I sometimes think Ben is a human dressed up as a dog he's so smart – and I know Sam's form teacher, Miss Scott, swears he understands most of the lessons – except maths!"*

CHAPTER SIXTEEN

THE TRAP IS MADE AND BAITED

Sam was pleased with his mobile 'phone, even if – as his mother had guessed – Ben was a bit put out that he couldn't use it.

However, it helped to keep Sam from thinking too much about the visit to his father's flat. Ben, being a dog – even if a very smart dog – found it quite hard to think about things several days ahead in the future and simply got on with his job of looking after Sam.

Between them they had most things quite well sorted out. Ben had learned the school routine very well and made sure that Sam had his school bag on the back of his chair and that no-one mucked it about. One or two boys had tried that and backed off pretty smartly when Ben grabbed them firmly by their jacket, trousers or even their hand.

Alice was also thinking hard, not just about the visit to the flat, but how to trap Sir John and deliver him to the police, so she had plenty to do.

Jack Riley had spent a day with his old friends in the Drugs Squad at Scotland Yard. To his relief he found that although the Squad had been reorganised he knew several of the people in charge of hunting down the drug racketeers.

As he told Alice that evening, it was just like old times.

"We are in luck" he explained. *"They know quite a lot about Sir John and a bit about how he uses the legal company that imports and exports wheat and barley and that sort of stuff as a cover for the drugs business, but they don't know enough to arrest him, get him convicted and sent to prison for the drugs offences, let alone for murder and they certainly don't know enough to pick up the people who work for him. In fact they have not listed Sam's father's death as murder – let alone that Sir John was the killer.*

What's more – the people who work for him are too scared to talk to the police, especially the ones who do know what happened to Sam's father.

Anyway, the police are pretty keen to help us, but they dare not take part in fooling him into giving himself away. You remember what it is like. The big boys in the drugs trade can afford the most expensive lawyers who can wreck a prosecution case in court if the police have, as the lawyers call it, 'obtained evidence by deception'.

Fortunately, we aren't the police and we are not acting under their instructions. They don't even have to know quite what we are up to.

All we have to worry about is making sure that sir John doesn't outsmart us and that Sam doesn't get hurt."

As usual, Alice was thinking hard. She raised one hand and Jack paused as she cut in.

"Yes. We talked about that the other night. You didn't like my idea of telling Sir John we had got the car he used to push Sam's father's car off the road. Well, I've thought of a way to do that, but I've got something even better here."

Alice then dug into her handbag and with something of a flourish brought out the 1812 Overture disc.

"This was one of the discs Sam brought back from his father's flat. But it has a bit of a surprise if you expect it to be great work by Tchaikovsky. Sam only listened to the first few minutes of this, so I think we had better put it on so we know just what is there. Where is your CD player?"

Jack took the disc, slipped it into the player and sat down as the music began. Then after a minute or so, the music died away and the voice of Sam's father took over.

The two of them sat listening as Sam's father described Sir John Munday's vast drug smuggling operation which he had hidden behind the perfectly respectable and proper business of his International Grain Transport and Trading Company. He listed the names of all Sir John's accomplices and contacts in Britain and overseas and how they used a network of foreign mobile 'phones to keep in touch, making it harder for the police in Britain to monitor their calls.

Then there was a pause before Sam's father continued. *"It is pretty frustrating. Munday is very smart. Although I know all this I have not got a shred of paper to prove it. It would be just my word against not just his, but those of all his people. They know on which side their bread is buttered. They would not risk their lives by turning against him. What I have to do now is to persuade my bosses at Television News to help me to set up some sort of sting operation to trap him."*

Sam's father's voice stopped and the music crashed out again.

Jack switched off the player. He and Alice sat silent, looking at each other for a minute or more.

"Alice," said Jack. *"Sir John Munday must have found out that the man he thought was one of his agents was really an investigative journalist who knew far too much for his own good – or Sir John's for that matter. Ben was right. We have to be careful. Sam could be in great danger if Sir John knew that this disc existed and that Sam had got it."*

After a moment or two Alice drew a deep breath. Then she spoke quite slowly.

"It is time we put pen to paper and drew up a plan. We have got the disc and we know about the dodgy car dealer in Islington. We know he was paid to get rid of the car that Munday used to push Sam's father's car off the road. I'll jot down some ideas on how we might use the information about the car. The idea is to get Sir John to Sam's father's flat. Then get the police ready to grab him once we have fooled him into incriminating himself. We can wire up the flat with concealed microphones and video cameras to help with that. Now, no talking. We will compare notes in half an hour."

Jack said nothing. He had seen Alice in that sort of mood before. She was a remarkably tough and very clever woman and he knew of no-one who had ever got the better of her.

He went into his office and came out with two note pads and pens, handed one of each to Alice and sat down at the table, hands in his lap and eyes closed for a few moments before beginning to write.

Alice sat for rather longer, frowning hard before she picked up her pen and began to set out columns with headings such as "WHAT WE KNOW", "WHAT SIR JOHN KNOWS" and "HOW TO BAIT THE TRAP".

Exactly half an hour later Alice put down her pen and said,

"Time's up. Let's see what you have got," as she handed her pad to Jack and took his in return.

Jack's plan was simple enough. He knew enough about the dodgy car dealer's crooked business to frighten him. He would go to the garage in Islington and tell him that Sir John was going to be told that the car had not been destroyed and he would be very angry so it would be best if the dealer disappeared for a couple of weeks. Of course the dealer would say it wasn't true. He would say the car had been destroyed, but Jack would tell him Sir John would not believe him, so he had better go to ground for a while. Anyway, as Jack put it,

"I'll put the frighteners on him," and Alice knew exactly what he meant.

Once the dealer had been got out of the way, Jack would 'phone sir John on one of the secret 'phone numbers which he used to stay in touch with his drug dealers to say that the car that had pushed Sam's father, Charles Turner's car off the road had not been destroyed and that he knew where it was.

Jack reckoned that Sir John would try to get hold of the dodgy car dealer and would be worried when he discovered that he had "done a runner". A day or two later Jack would call again to say he had the car and would sell it back to Sir John for £100,000.

Alice's plan was even simpler, but fitted nicely with Jack's. It was to call Sir John on his drug dealers' 'phone number and play part of the recording of Sam's father listing the details of the drug business organisation.

"Just that and nothing else," she explained to Jack. *"He'll be worried by that, because it would prove that someone else knew what Sam's father had discovered."*

Then, the next day Alice would ring him again to say she knew where the disc was hidden in Sam's father's flat and for £100,000 would show him how to find it. If he didn't pay up she would hand it over to the police.

"And," she added, *"I would tell him to bring another £100,000 for the keys to his car."*

Jack smiled. *"That's fine – but we have to tell Sam. He might well have his own ideas on how we do this. We have to get his agreement. We have to see the flat. And we have to have a plan to make Sir John really incriminate himself before the police move in to arrest him. And we have to get the police on side and ready to do their bit."*

"And that's enough for tonight," declared Alice. *"Now can we have supper?"*

Sam was finding it hard to concentrate on his school work and even Ben, who was a true Labrador at heart and normally able to push problems not just to the back of his mind, but pretty well right out of it, found he kept worrying about what Alice and Jack were planning.

Ben felt a bit out of his depth. Being a dog he could sometimes be aware of dangers that humans might miss. His nose was always twitching, picking up any unusual scent that might mean danger. He could even feel vibrations through his feet that we humans with our socks and shoes never do, and pick up sounds too high pitched for our ears. But none of that was any help to him to guard his master against the danger which worried him. He knew that Sir John Munday had killed Sam's father because he knew about the drugs business (which Ben only half understood) and that now Sam had discovered what his father had found out, Sir John might even kill Sam.

His only comfort was that he felt sure that Alice and Jack were at least as clever as Sir John. She sometimes reminded him of his old master Boris, which made him feel sad too, so all in all, his tail sometimes drooped and his ears hung down in the way that a Labrador's do when he is unsure and insecure.

Sam felt his life was still swinging up and down as it had begun to do ever since his mother had left his father to live with George, then even worse when he had woken up in hospital to find his father was dead and that he would never walk again. Finding Ben had been wonderful, finding that he could talk was even better, but now everything was swinging around again with Alice and Jack entering his life. Nor did he like being untruthful to his mother and George and he was certain that his sister, Sophie knew something very strange was going on.

There was nothing he could do but grit his teeth, try to concentrate on his lessons and wait for Alice to pick him up on Saturday.

It was a great relief to Sam when he found on Friday morning there was a text message from Alice on his mobile 'phone.

"Sam, I'll pick you up at 8.30 on Saturday. Don't forget the keys to the flat and don't forget that your mother thinks you are going to Canine Partners. I've told Clive Baker that if your mother rings there he is to pretend that you are out on a training exercise with another boy and his dog and then to 'phone me... Alice."

Sam read the message aloud to Ben who seemed cheered up when he knew Alice would pick them up next day.

They were ready in good time and sharp on the dot of 8.30, Alice was at the door. After the exchange of a few words of greeting with Sam's mother, she ushered the boy and the dog into her car. As they set off Sam said,

"I thought Jack was coming."

"He is," replied Alice. *"He is waiting down the road as I didn't want to explain him to your mother. If you can avoid making up a tale or telling a porkie, you should, because you have to remember all the ones you tell or you'll get caught out. Oh yes, did you borrow the keys to the flat?"*

"Yes," said Sam. *"Ben reminded me. Oh look, there's Jack."*

Alice stopped to pick up Jack and once they were on their way again he turned to Sam.

"I hope this is going to be okay Sam. I'll tell you the plan, but there is one snag. I'm having a bit of trouble with getting the police signed up to help us.

My friends are all okay, but their boss says it is asking a lot to put a dozen or more men, some of them armed, on to an operation planned by a pair of retired intelligence spooks, a boy and a dog.

But let's talk about that when we get to the flat. I know the way – I was around the place yesterday and by the look of it, it is ideal. With the river right behind it and only one lift, one set of stairs and one fire escape, there are not many ways Sir John could try to get away without running into a policeman."

Alice just sighed and turned to speak to Sam.

"Jack thinks of most things Sam. All we have to do now is to invent some

good bait to persuade the police to turn up to our party next week. But we will think about that later."

Sam noticed that Alice drove much more like his father had done than either his mother or George. She rarely braked hard or accelerated harshly, but the car seemed to cut through the traffic smoothly and easily.

Ben simply snuggled down on the floor, and as dogs do at such times, drifted off to sleep, but with one ear cocked for anything which might mean danger and a nose ever watchful for the scent of either danger or food.

No one felt much like talking and the journey passed mostly in silence until they were approaching Sam's father's flat, when Alice began to look for a place to park.

"But we are still a little way from the flat," Sam pointed out.

Alice smiled. *"I know, but we don't want to all arrive together. People are more likely to notice the four of us together than if we split up. You take the key Sam and go with Ben, let yourselves in and leave the door on the latch. Jack and I will follow and keep you in sight and just come into the flat."*

Jack was smiling to himself, thinking that Alice had not changed a bit in all the years he had known her. Sam was thinking that she just seemed naturally to take charge, rather like his father, whilst Ben thought she was really very much like his old master Boris.

Ten minutes later and they were all in the flat where Alice opened her bag, pulled out milk, a packet of tea bags and another of biscuits.

"Time for tea and a biscuit," she observed. *"Now where is the kettle Sam?"*

Ben, who had been sniffing around the flat, looked up at the word 'biscuit', and Sam, who had been deep in memories of his father, came out from his thoughts to ask,

"What next then Alice?"

Within a few minutes as they talked, the plan began to take firm shape. Alice told Sam and Ben how Sir John would be lured to the flat by the 'phone calls about his car and the voice of Sam's father from the 1812 disc. Then a plain clothed police officer concealed in a van parked outside would signal the rest of the police to move forward and surround the flat. Alice, wearing a concealed microphone and transmitter, would let Sir John in, whilst Jack hid in the bedroom.

"*Yes, that's all very well,*" interrupted Sam, "*but if you want to really surprise Sir John, so that he does give the game away, shouldn't I appear and say something like 'you killed my father'?*"

"*Yes,*" said Alice, "*I think it would be best if you and Ben hid in the big cupboard in the kitchen-living room. That is where I will ask Sir John to hand over the money for the disc and the keys to the car that he used to push your father's car off the road.*

I'll wind him up," she promised. "*At the right moment I'll give you a shout to come out of the cupboard and shout something like 'YOU KILLED MY FATHER.' That's when I'll tell him we are not going to take him just for a couple of hundred thousand pounds, but at least a million a year.*

If I have judged him right – as a coward and a bully – Sir John will just about 'go ape' and say more than enough to convict himself which is where the police move in – and we can go home for dinner."

Sam and Jack had listened intently to every word that Alice had uttered. Ben, sitting beside Sam with his nose on the boy's lap, could feel, let alone read his thought. He was utterly bowled over by the way Alice – the little old lady – had become a brutally tough, totally fearless plotter of the plan to put Munday where he belonged – in jail.

"*But Alice,*" Sam half whispered. "*Suppose it doesn't work like that. Suppose it all goes wrong?*"

"*Then we have to think quickly – and Jack has to think very quickly.*

Now let's make sure there is enough room for you and Ben in the cupboard and somewhere for Jack to hide. Then the job's done for today and we can go home. After that it is up to Jack to sort out his chums in the police so they can do their bit and for the two of us to make the 'phone calls to Sir John Munday."

Ben found it all quite hard to follow, but he knew Alice was now the leader of the pack hunting down Sir John, whilst his job was to protect Sam. Between them, Alice, Sam and Jack, they would set the trap and bait it well. Sir John was the rat and that was that.

No one spoke much on the journey home until, as they approached Tring, Sam made sure he had got his story about having been to Canine Partners off pat, ready to tell his mother.

"*And,*" Alice added. "*You could say that Clive Baker and I were very pleased* with your help – and Ben's," she added hastily, "and we might want you to help again next Saturday evening."

A few minutes later, just before they got to the road where Sam lived, Alice stopped to let Jack Riley out of the car saying, "It's easier not to have to explain who you are Jack if Sam's mother or George should see us. There'll be enough explaining to do after next Saturday!"

Minutes later, they stopped at Sam's home. Alice took him to the door, told Sam's mother that they had had a successful day and wished him goodnight.

Sam was quite quiet at dinner, but assured his mother, George and Sophie that he had had a very good day and that Ben was wonderful at showing the other dogs what to do, before excusing himself to go to his room to catch up on his homework.

Once the door was shut he looked hard at Ben.

"Ben," said Sam. "I think I am half excited and half scared – and sometimes I wish that I had never found out the car crash wasn't an accident..."

"But you did find out Master," interrupted Ben. The boy looked at the dog for a long time, then slowly he spoke again.

"As usual Ben, you're right. I did find out and I can't just unfind it out, so between us, Alice and Jack, we have to get it right. But I am still a bit scared that it might go wrong."

They both sat silently looking at each other for a long time before Ben, as he so often did, put his paws on the boy's lap and looked straight into his eyes.

"Master, I don't think Sir John is nearly as clever as the old lady, Alice. I'm sure that even if we haven't done things like this before, she and Jack certainly have. I think it is time for bed."

Back at Jack Riley's home, he and Alice were still sitting at the table plotting out exactly what everybody now had to do from the 'phone calls to Sir John to finalising the arrangements with the police.

It was late when they finished. Jack finally said, "I think that is just about as good a plan as we could have, but ..."

And both he and Alice chorused together,

"But no plan can ever survive contact with reality."

And they both burst out laughing.

"What's more Jack," laughed Alice, "we have never had a boy and dog help us with a plan before, but there's nothing more to do tonight. It's time for bed."

Next day, just as they had agreed with Sam and Ben, Alice and Jack began to set the trap.

Somewhat to his surprise, Sam enjoyed a good night's sleep, but he had scarcely lifted his head off the pillow in the morning before he began to think about Alice and Jack and their plans to trap Sir John.

They, of course, were thinking hard not only about how to get Sir John to Sam's father's flat, but just how between the four of them, they would so unsettle and frighten Sir John that he would say enough to incriminate himself not just as a drug dealer, but as a murderer too.

"Let's make sure we get this right," said Alice. "I'll kick off by 'phoning Sir John and playing enough of the information hidden by Sam's father on the 1812 Overture disc to give him a fright. I need one of our old friends to help by putting that on to a mobile 'phone that he can't trace and then calling him – and I guess that will take until Tuesday."

Jack nodded. "And I've got to go to see that dodgy car dealer, put the frighteners on him and get him out of town. I'll start on that on Monday. We can't risk Sir John finding out that the car really was destroyed. That would screw things up completely. He has to believe we have it. Once I have fixed the car dealer, I'll call Sir John on one of those secret 'phone numbers to kid him we have got the car that would link him to the murder of Sam's father and offer to sell it to him for a hundred grand. I know a hundred thousand pounds is a lot of money, but if I asked anything less, he would be suspicious. If we were crooks and if we really did have it, that's the sort of money we would ask."

Alice thought quietly for a minute or so before she spoke again.

"Okay. Do that on Wednesday. Tell him you'll ring him again to tell him where to take the money – that is, to the flat."

"Then I'll ring him on Thursday to say I understand he is going to meet you on Saturday at the flat, and I'll be there too, so he had better bring another hundred grand to buy the disc – and no funny business."

Jack smiled. "I'm almost beginning to feel sorry for him."

Alice cut him short. "Well don't. He deserves everything he is going to get." Her voice hardened and both she and Jack realised not just how much they detested this man, although they had never met him, but how dangerous he might be.

"And the next thing is. What happens when we get him to the flat?"

Over the rest of the morning the two of them went over and over again every detail until at last, Alice looked up from her notepad and said.

"That's it. We can't go much further. We can only guess at what Sir John will do, but we must be ready for him to carry a gun or turn violent and we have to protect the boy. Can you borrow a bullet proof vest for him and have you still got a gun for yourself?"

"You can rely on me," replied Jack. *"And now it's time for lunch. It's Sunday, so Sam will be at home today. Why don't you text Sam on his mobile and we'll meet him in the park this afternoon?"*

Back at his home, Sam had been trying to concentrate on some school work, but he couldn't avoid thinking about Alice and Jack and the plan to catch Sir John.

Being a dog, Ben found that much easier to do and he was dozing quietly beside Sam's chair when the ping-pong from Sam's 'phone woke him as Alice's text message arrived. In a moment he was wide awake looking at Sam as he read the text message.

Sam told Ben what was going on. *"Alice wants to meet us in the park in an hour's time. All I've got to do is make sure neither my mother, nor George nor Sophie come too. I'll say I'm just taking you for a leak and a run while I swot up those history dates for school."* And he set to texting his reply to Alice.

An hour later all four of them, Sam, Ben, Alice and Jack were at the corner table in the cafe and Alice began briefing Sam about the final details of their plan.

Sam and Ben listened quietly as Alice explained how she and Jack would make the 'phone calls to get Sir John to the flat.

"Suppose he doesn't come?" asked Sam.

"Oh, he will," said Jack. *"He'll be on edge because of hearing your father's voice listing all his secret dealers; then after I've rung him he'll try to get hold of that dodgy car dealer and he'll find he's done a runner – and I'll make sure he has. I'll put the fear of God into him and he'll be out of town for a week at least. That will all work.*

It's the next bit – when we get him to the flat – that worries me. He'll probably have a gun on him – but so will I and I'll get you a bullet proof vest just to be safe. This is what we think we will do."

Alice was watching Sam's face as Jack said, *"Sam, we have been through most of this before, but I want to be really sure you know just what we are going to do. We will drop you and Ben off by Wapping tube station. One of my friends will be there and he will drive Alice and me to your father's flat and take the car away. That will give us time whilst you are making your way from the station to make sure that neither Sir John nor any of his friends are hanging around. In fact, the police should be trailing him to let us know if he is trying anything on.*

By the time you get to the flat Alice will already be there. I'll be in the pub over the road and I'll follow you up to the flat a minute or two later to make sure no one is following you."

Sam sat thinking this was all like a gangster film whilst Ben was trying hard to remember it all.

Alice smiled at the boy. *"You know Sam, Jack and I have done this sort of thing before, usually with rather more awkward people than Sir John. Don't worry. I'll let you in and then, as Jack says, he will come up in a minute or so.*

We will be there an hour before Sir John is due to arrive so I'll bring something to eat – and you had better remember something for Ben and – oh yes – Ben – don't forget to have a leak on the way from the station because you won't be able to go out again until it is all over. Anyway, we will have time to check that the flat is wired for sound, and so will I be, so we will have a record of everything Sir John says.

Now Jack, you explain what happens after that."

Jack flattened out a plan of the flat on the cafe table pointing out with his pen the big cupboard in the sitting room.

"Do you remember when we were in the flat yesterday we said you two will be in the cupboard. Alice will make sure it is really dusted. We don't want you sneezing at the wrong time. I will be in the bedroom.

There will be a couple of plain clothed policemen hanging around outside the pub and they will call me as soon as Sir John arrives. That is when you and Ben duck into the cupboard.

Alice will let him in. The police will move in to take control of the lift, the stairs and be at the bottom of the fire escape in case he tries to do a runner that way.

As Alice said, she will wind up Sir John a bit about selling him the 1812 disc. That will be in the disc player so that he can hear it and Alice will tell him she wants £200,000 in cash for the disc and the car.

That's when I walk in – with some car keys in my hand and say something like – 'drug dealing is one thing, but murder is another and your car is full of your DNA and the nearside is smeared with paint from Charles Turner's car which you pushed off the road to kill him – which is why his son wants to talk to you.'

That is when you and Ben come out of the cupboard. He will scream his head off – and I'll call in the police to take him away."

Ben had sat motionless, except for his eyes which had gone back and forth from Jack to Alice while the long furrow over his head became deeper and deeper as he struggled to follow everything Jack and Alice were saying. In the wild, packs of wild dogs and their cousins the wolves, organise the pack to trap their prey, but this was a really complicated trap and Ben was beginning to wonder if he and Sam were part of the bait?

Sam looked very thoughtful too and he took a very deep breath before he asked, very quietly,

"Isn't Sir John going to be very angry and very frightened when he realises that he has walked into a trap? And doesn't that mean he might do something violent or silly?"

Jack nodded. *"That's why I will be armed and why you will be wearing a bullet proof waistcoat, and why there will be plenty of police around the place."*

"Now I don't think there is much more to say or do at present. Alice and I will keep you in touch with what we are up to by text messages to your mobile and we will stitch up some yarn to convince your mother that Alice should come to collect you on Saturday. We will have our work to do during the week and we will let you know how it all goes."

"As usual Sam, you head off home first with Ben and we will hang around here until you are almost home."

There was nothing more to say, except as Sam remembered just in time, to thank Alice for his tea and with Ben watchful as ever for any dangers, they headed for home.

About a hundred yards before they reached Sam's home Ben shot ahead of the wheelchair, then turned to face Sam, going down on his belly looking up at his master.

"What's wrong?" asked Sam. Ben looked hard at him.

"Master. You must not let Sophie, George or your mother know you are worried about anything. Just do everything as normal. It is Sunday today and it is school tomorrow. You have done your homework so you should not go straight to your room after dinner. Just talk as usual to the others for a while. It will be time enough next Sunday to think how we explain all this without giving away my secret."

"You are a wise old dog," said Sam. *"Thank you. I might even drop a forkful of my dinner tonight for you."*

CHAPTER SEVENTEEN

THE WAITING

For Sam the next few days dragged slowly by and there was little Ben could do to help him, except to make sure he was up, dressed, had breakfast, got to school on time and paid attention in class.

Ben could always tell when Sam's mind drifted away from a lesson in class to begin to worry about what might happen at the flat on Saturday. When that happened he would give Sam a nudge and whisper very quietly, *"Pay attention Sam."*

It was very different for Alice and Jack. Jack had to go into Islington in North London on Monday to visit the dodgy car dealer at Water's Autos to make sure he would be well out of the way before Jack told Sir John that his car had not been destroyed.

That did not take long. Jack soon found Water's Autos and started to look at the second hand cars, and it was not very many moments before the dealer, John Waters, was at his side.

"Looking for anything special?" he asked.

"Well yes," replied Jack. *"How about a silver 2009 BMW with a bit of damage on the nearside? One that used to be owned by International Grain*

Transport and Trading...?"

Waters, the car dealer, looked around as if to make sure no one was in earshot before turning back to Jack.

"No, I ain't – nothing like that..." but Jack cut him short.

"But Sir John thinks you have. That's why I'm asking you. He thinks you didn't burn it and get it crushed for scrap. He thinks you might try to blackmail him. And I think he will be coming to see you – or perhaps he might send one of his friends to see you ..."

By now Waters was white with anger and fear.

"What the Hell has any of that got to do with you – and anyway, who the Hell are you?"

Jack smiled. *"Just call me Jack. I could be your friend and I've got some friendly advice for you. Don't contact Sir John. That would be very dangerous for you. I know all about the car and about Sir John. And I know quite a lot about you, but I don't want anything unpleasant to happen to you – or your girl friend. So I've brought you both a present."*

Jack pulled out an envelope from his pocket, opened it and gave the contents to Waters.

"Here are two tickets for the Eurostar to Paris and a booking for a nice room at The Metropole Hotel for a week. It's all arranged and paid for. The train leaves at nine o'clock tonight. So just get packed and get out of town or something really nasty might happen to you. Don't muck me about. Some of my friends will be watching you. Do a runner while you've still got a whole skin. It will be safe for you to come back in a week's time. Until then, all the best. Cheerio."

And before Waters could say a word, Jack was gone.

Whilst Jack was putting the frighteners on Waters, the dodgy dealer, Alice was preparing a fright for Sir John. With a few 'phone calls she had arranged to fix a taped message to go with part of Sam's father Charles' account of Sir John's drugs business on the 1812 Overture disc.

That evening Alice and Jack agreed to 'phone him on one of his secret 'phone numbers used by his top drug dealers and play the tape to him on Tuesday morning.

"That's enough for today Jack," she said. *"I'll text Sam to say it's going well and then it's time for dinner."*

Sam was pleased to read Alice's message although it simply said,

"All going well. Will text you again tomorrow. Alice."

Next morning, however, Sir John Munday was far from pleased at his call from Alice. He had not been expecting a call on his secret 'phone number which he thought was known only to one of the top managers of his drugs business.

He was even less pleased to hear a woman's voice he did not recognise.

"Good morning Sir John. I have got a message for you from one of your former employees."

As Sir John looked as though the 'phone had bitten him, Alice continued,

"You remember Charles Turner don't you?"

There was a moment's silence and then the voice of Sam's father taken from the 1812 Overture disc began setting out what he had discovered about Sir John's drugs racket. Then with a click the call ended.

First anger, then fear left Sir John shaking as he slammed down the 'phone.

Then Jack made another 'phone call. This time to The Metropole Hotel in Paris to confirm that Waters, the dodgy car dealer, had booked in.

Jack rubbed his hands in glee.

"We'll let Sir John stew tonight and I'll call him in the morning to ask him if he would like to buy his car back. In the meantime, we can text Sam again to let him know all is going well."

It was Ben who heard the 'ping' of a text message on Sam's phone as they were struggling through the throng of other pupils at Tring School heading for home at four o'clock. He waited until they were well clear of the school, then said very quietly to Sam,

"There's a message on your 'phone – I heard it as we were leaving school."

Sam stopped in his wheelchair and pulled out the 'phone to read out the message.

"Sam and Ben: Sir John very worried. Dodgy car dealer in Paris. All going well."

"Where is Paris?" asked Ben. Sam laughed.

"Oh dear dog – you haven't been doing your geography homework – it's in France – far enough away."

"Humph," sniffed Ben. *"No one ever told me. Sometimes you humans take us dogs for granted."*

Sam suddenly realised that all too often he forgot that Ben was a dog and gave his ears a rub.

"Oh, I am so sorry Ben. You're right. I do sometimes forget. Let's go to the park for an extra run."

The idea of an extra run got Ben's tail up and wagging.

"I think we are both worried about all this business."

Despite everything, both Sam and Ben enjoyed their dinner and as there wasn't much homework, Sam watched 'TOP GEAR' which always made him laugh, before going to his room.

Before getting into bed he sent a quick text back to Alice.

"Thanks for your text. Will you ring my mother about us going to London on Saturday?"

Alice and Jack were still talking after dinner when Sam's text arrived. Alice read it and passed it to Jack.

"Oh Lord," he muttered. *"What a useless pair we are – and what a good job the boy has got brains. We forgot all about that, so you had better cook up a story with Clive at Canine Partners for him to tell Sam's mother. That is the first thing to do tomorrow."*

On Wednesday, it didn't take long to fix a story with Clive at Canine Partners, nor for him to 'phone Sam's mother to tell her that Alice would pick Sam up on Saturday to go to a meeting in London to publicise what Canine Partners could do to help disabled people.

"Sam and Ben are such good examples," Clive told Sam's mother. *"You should be proud of them."*

After that it was time for Jack to 'phone Sir John.

"*Good morning Sir John,*" he began. But before he could get any further Sir John was shouting at him.

"*Who the Hell are you? What do you want?*"

"*To sell you a car. It is a lovely BMW saloon. The only thing wrong with it is some accident damage on the nearside – and inside there is plenty of your DNA. How about a hundred thousand pounds for it? I'll call tomorrow to tell you where to bring the money.*"

By now Sir John was far more angry than he was frightened.

Within minutes he was on the 'phone to John Waters, the dodgy car dealer in Islington.

"*Get me John Waters,*" he snapped at the girl who answered the 'phone, "*and get him quick.*"

"*I'm sorry,*" came the reply. "*He isn't here. He's taken a week off.*"

Sir John butted in. "*Where is he? I need to speak to him.*"

"*I really don't know and it doesn't help shouting at me. He just said he needed to go abroad for a week and he took his girl friend with him the night before last. That's all I know.*"

Sir John said no more. As he put the 'phone down his rage and fright began to change into an icy cold determination to get even with Waters and the man and woman demanding money from him. And that won't be easy, he told himself, but the stakes were getting high. He had dealt with blackmailers before and he knew that he would have to agree to meet them. They knew far too much to risk pretending it would all just blow over. "*I'll wait. They'll call back.*" he muttered and tried to concentrate on his work.

In the meantime, Alice and Jack were enjoying a cup of tea and texting Sam again, just to let him know everything was still going to plan.

"*Then,*" said Alice. "*There's not much to do until tomorrow. I think Sir John is beginning to feel the pressure – we can leave him to stew.*"

Just as planned, Alice 'phoned Sir John on Thursday morning. He let the 'phone ring for a moment or two before gingerly picking it up. Alice put on her sweetest voice.

"*Hello Sir John. I hope you weren't annoyed by my friend Jack wanting to sell you a second hand car, but it is a very nice one. Well, you know it well enough don't you? We will meet you at Charles Turner's flat in Wapping. You*" know where that is because you have been there – twice in fact I think. You were looking for his papers about your business, but you didn't know where to look, but I'll show you. My friend Jack will bring your car keys and we will tell you where to find that too. And you, Sir John, will bring two hundred thousand pounds – that is one hundred thousand pounds for the car and one hundred thousand pounds for the disc and we can all go home happy. I will confirm the time tomorrow. Don't go poking around anywhere near the flat in the meantime. That would be a terrible mistake. You don't know who we are, but we know all about you. Bye, bye."

That night when Sam got another text from Alice, it just said,

"All still going well. Our friend is very worried now. We will pick you up at 4.00 pm on Saturday and be at Wapping by 6.00 pm and he will arrive at 7.00 pm. Sleep well."

Sam read it out to Ben in the park on the way home from school. Ben sniffed,

"It's all very well for Alice and Jack, but I know you worry about it all Master."

"I do," the boy confessed. "I'll just be glad when it is all over."

Friday dragged by for Sam. Whatever else he was doing, every now and again the thought of what was to happen on Saturday night came into his thoughts.

Again and again he had to tell himself that Alice and Jack knew what they were doing; that the trap was well and cunningly laid and Sir John was not just a truly bad character, but that he had killed his father and left him stuck in a wheelchair for the rest of his life.

Being a dog, Ben saw things much more simply. Alice was his friend who had helped him when he was all alone in England. Jack was her friend and Sam was his Master. He was part of their pack and he would always be loyal to them whatever happened.

He wished he could do more to comfort and encourage Sam for he often caught the boy's thoughts and knew how worried he was. All he could do was to whisper very quietly,

"It will soon be all over and everyone will be so pleased – and you will be alright. Alice and Jack and I will make sure of that."

Fortunately, it was lasagne for dinner on Friday and that was a favourite for both Sam and George who told a very funny story about his day and the evening went by very quickly. Even so, Sam's mother noticed the boy seemed tense, but thought it must be about his new role in helping to publicise Canine Partners.

On Saturday morning it would have been more true to say that Ben took Sam for a run in the park rather than the other way around, and they both needed to be cleaned up (and Ben loved a bath, then his rub dry with his big towel and a good brush).

By the time they were done and Sam had quietly pocketed the keys to the flat, it was almost 4.00 pm. Dead on time, Alice was at the door to pick them up. As usual she had left Jack at the end of the road to avoid any extra explanations about who he was.

As Alice had told Sam before, *"the fewer stories and porkies you have to make up and tell, the less likely it is that you will be caught out."*

On the way into London no one spoke very much. Jack reminded Sam of the plan and assured both him and Alice that the police would be there ready to arrest Sir John when they were called in, or if he tried to make a run for it.

As they reached Wapping station, Sam handed the keys to Jack who said,

"Good thinking – but I had some more made just in case, thank you."

Both Sam and Ben were glad of the few minutes walk to the flat where Alice and Jack had already made a pot of tea.

"Not long now," said Alice. *"Now, let's make sure that this bullet proof vest fits Sam. We don't want him to get hurt."*

Sam and Ben checked their places in the cupboard. Alice checked her concealed microphones and recorder. Jack checked in with the police on his radio and with all as prepared as could be there was just time for tea and biscuits before the police called Jack.

"Your man has just parked his car and is coming into the flats."

"Thanks," replied Jack. *"Ben, Sam – into the cupboard. I'll be in the*

bedroom – he'll be here in a minute."

Alice was ready and opened the door as soon as the bell rang.

"Good evening, Sir John – how nice to see you and with a nice fat briefcase full of money I see."

Sir John laid the briefcase on the table and stepped closer to Alice.

"I don't like blackmailers and I don't like being taken for a fool. Where is the disc? Where is the car and the keys? Don't mess me about."

"Oh the disc," smiled Alice. *"It's in the player of course – it starts rather nicely with the 1812 Overture – listen,"* as she turned on the disc player.

Within moments there was the voice of Sam's father, Charles Turner, listing the details of Sir John's drugs racket.

"That's enough. Okay – I'm no fool and I know you will have copied that disc – but I tell you this. If you ever try to blackmail me again – then Turner's boy, Sam, will be dead meat. He'll go the same way as his father – a pity he didn't go at the same time as his father. And you and your friend might have a nasty accident too".

Jack decided it was time for him to join the action.

Opening the bedroom door he stepped into the living room and according to plan, waving a set of car keys at Sir John.

"How about a hundred grand for these? Cheap at the price. The disc would only send you down for drug dealing. The car would get you for murder. Cheap at the price, I would say."

When Sir John spoke his voice had dropped a little and became icy calm.

"Now, just exactly who the Hell are you? I don't like doing business with strangers."

"Strangers?" said Alice. *"We are just your friends. We are giving you the first chance to buy that nice BMW car and this disc, at a very reasonable price. After all, someone else – perhaps a newspaper – might give us a better price – but we thought that it might be nice to do a deal now, tonight, with you. Come on – let's get on with it. You know you pushed Turner's car off the road and that the car would prove it."*

Suddenly, Sir John sounded angry.

"That's enough. I trusted Turner. He ratted on me – the miserable treacherous bastard – he got what he deserved."

In the cupboard, Sam was rigid with anger. *"Master – now – now – go on."* Ben pushed him against the door which swung open.

"God – it's that bloody boy," shouted Sir John.

"Yes, it's me – and I know for certain you killed my father. You did, didn't you?" The words tumbled out of Sam's lips. *"You killed him – you murderer."*

Sir John scarcely looked at Sam as he pulled a gun out of the briefcase on the table.

"Shut up boy – shut up. And you two get over there against that wall. Put the keys on the table – and boy – take the disc out of the play – go on, quick, or you'll go the same way of your father – put it on the table with the keys."

Sir John's eyes darted back and forth between Alice and Jack and Sam.

"Come on, move – and move quickly." Sam put the disc on the table.

"You boy – go over there away from those two. Come on – the keys – quick."

Jack threw the keys alongside the disc. Sir John picked them both up without lowering the gun or taking his eyes off Alice and Jack.

Ben had kept quiet – still only half out of the cupboard, watching and concentrating on picking up Jack's unspoken thoughts.

"This is not going quite right. If I pull my gun, there'll be a shoot-out and Alice or Sam will get hurt. I'll play for time. The police will be here in a moment."

Indeed, at that very moment there was a crash at the door and a shout,

"Armed police – open the door."

Then the crack of a gunshot as a bullet smashed open the door lock.

Even as the police kicked the door open, Sir John had grabbed Sam's chair, pulling it in front of himself with one hand, holding the gun in the other and starting to back towards the fire escape door behind him.

More police came rushing up the steps. There was now only one escape for Sir John. The River Thames was forty feet below, but he was a powerful swimmer and he had no intention of leaving quietly.

Neither Sir John, Alice nor Jack had noticed Ben, who had slid on his belly across from the cupboard, ears down, his eyes fixed on Sir John, as he leaned back on the opening bar of the fire escape door and backed out onto the platform.

Now Sam too realised it was all going wrong. He tried to grab Sir John's gun, but missed. Before the police, who had burst in, had a chance to sum up who Sir John was, Sir John tipped over Sam's wheelchair sending the boy sprawling across the floor. He turned the gun onto Sam shouting,

"I should have got you when I got your father."

But before he or the police could fire, there was a terrible growl of rage and Ben catapulted himself full stretch in a colossal leap over Sam and the wheelchair, straight at Sir John's chest.

The impact sent Sir John reeling backwards. The gun went off harmlessly into the air and man and dog tumbled together into the cold dark river below as Jack and one of the policemen, who had burst into the flat, rushed out onto the fire escape platform.

Alice was first to speak. *"Sam are you alright?"*

"I think so," stuttered Sam. *"But what about Ben? Is he in the river?"*

"I can see them both," Jack shouted. *"I think they are heading for a little beach about a hundred yards downstream. Quick, call the boys outside to get there – ready for him – and call the River Police."*

Between the two of them, Alice and Jack picked Sam up off the floor and bundled him into his wheelchair. Sam coughed and then regained his voice. *"Come on, let's get there,"* and he headed for the door.

Down in the dark river, Sir John had struck out, not for the beach where the police were heading, but for the other side of the river, not realising that Ben was close behind him.

Suddenly, he heard a voice in his head. *"You killed my Master's father. Now I will kill you."* In a moment Ben was on his shoulders, pressing him down into the cold River Thames.

"Get off! Get off!" Sir John screamed. Again he heard the dog's voice in his head.

"No, Sir John. No. You killed my Master's father and I am going to kill you."

Ben's weight and the drag of Sir John's sodden clothes were too much for him. Struggle as he did, it was never a fight he could win. His screams bubbled into silence as the dog held his head beneath the water.

It did not take long. Then once Ben was sure that Sir John was drowned, he began to drag his dead body towards the little beach at the foot of the river embankment. There were men shouting, blue lights and torches flashing as he reached the shallows and began to drag Sir John's body out of the water.

Friendly hands grabbed Ben's collar and pulled him up out of the water. Others caught hold of Sir John's jacket and dragged his body onto the footpath.

"*Christ!*" said one of the police. "*I thought the dog had saved him, but I think he's dead.*"

Ben barked. Not threatening, nor warning barks, but pleasure barks. He shook himself, sending showers of water over everyone. He knew he must not speak. There were too many people, especially police about, but he could – and he did – wag his tail. Then on the impulse of the moment, to the astonishment of the police officers, he lifted his leg over Sir John's body in a final calculated insult to the drug racketeer and killer of his Master's father.

That done, Ben sat quietly, good as gold, beside a friendly looking, even if slightly shocked policeman, as the sirens and blue lights announced the arrival of even more police cars. Then through it all, Ben spotted Sam thrashing along the path in his wheelchair with Alice and Jack close beside him. In a moment, Ben was standing up to him, forepaws on his lap.

"*I caught him Master,*" Ben whispered. Sam could hardly speak.

"*Oh Ben, Ben,*" he gasped. "*What happened?*"

"*I drowned him Master,*" said Ben, very quietly. "*Master. I am hungry. You wouldn't have a Bonio in your pocket would you? Then could we go home? Alice and Jack will have to explain to your mother why I am soaking wet and what we have been doing? I hope she will not be cross.*"

"*Don't worry Ben,*" said Sam. "*They can't charge a dog with murder. I think you are quite safe. You are a great dog. I just might have a Bonio for you.*"

THE END